ABOUT THE COVER

Olaf M. Brauner (1869-1947) first visited the Isles of Shoals in 1892 on vacation from the Boston Museum School. Celia Thaxter took a liking to the young artist and invited him to her Appledore salon where she introduced him to Childe Hassam and other talented American impressionists inspired by the beauty of the Isles. Recognizing Olaf's ties to Norway, Celia also introduced him to the daughter of a Norwegian Shoals fisherman; a few years later they were married. His wife Nikoline posed for several of Brauner's paintings, including the 30 x 36-inch oil on canvas, "The Lily White Wraith" (1914). The subject of this painting strongly suggests an eighteenth century tale of pirate Captain Scott who deserted his mistress on the Shoals and never returned. Her expectant, wan, sea-cloaked figure still is said to haunt the barren shores. The publisher is indebted to Karen Johnson Boyd, granddaughter of Olaf Brauner, for allowing the reproduction of this painting on the cover of THE ISLAND QUEEN.

Also by Julia Older

POETRY
Higher Latitudes
A Little Wild
Oonts & Others

FICTION
Blues for a Black Cat
  And Other Stories (translations)

NONFICTION
Celia Thaxter Selected Writings
Appalachian Odyssey
Endometriosis
Nature Walks in the Lakes Region
  of New Hampshire

THE ISLAND QUEEN

THE ISLAND QUEEN

Celia Thaxter of the Isles of Shoals

JULIA OLDER

APPLEDORE BOOKS
Hancock, New Hampshire

PUBLISHED SEPTEMBER 1994
SECOND PRINTING, JULY 1998

THE ISLAND QUEEN

Printed in 10 point Palatino
by Book Press, Inc.
Brattleboro VT
United States of America

ISBN 0-9627162-2-7

Library of Congress Cataloging - in - Publication
Library of Congress Catalogue Card Number: LC94-070760

Author's Note

The trial of Louis Wagner is based on actual trial transcripts, court records, and newspaper accounts. My gratitude to the New Hampshire State Historical Library, to the Portsmouth Public Library, and the Portsmouth Atheneum for making available these and other materials.

Several major insights into Celia's life were offered by Rosamond Thaxter (her granddaughter) who generously shared early reminiscences and impressions with me.

My appreciation to Donna Titus for sharing her thoughts about Celia, and her knowledge of the Isles of Shoals. Thanks also to Heather Gendron for her creative computing skills and patience with those who lack them.

THE ISLAND QUEEN was written in part at Yaddo in Saratoga Springs, New York, and at the Virginia Center for the Creative Arts. I'm most thankful for their support.

Quoted material includes excerpts from: William Shakespeare, *ROMEO AND JULIET* (Act II, Scene II); Celia Thaxter, "The Sandpiper," "Land-Locked," "Schumann's Sonata in A Minor;" Robert Browning, "Mertoun's Song;" a fragment by Sappho (c 612 BC); Charles Dickens, *DAVID COPPERFIELD* (opening); John Greenleaf Whittier, "Lines on Leaving Appledore" (from a letter to Celia published posthumously).

The wild wind raves, the tide runs high,
As up and down the beach we flit, —
One little sandpiper and I.

CONTENTS

Carefree and Unafraid

1

Celia bounded out of bed, pulled up the window sash, and stuck her head way out. The sun was peeking over the sea and setting fire to the low shoals on Duck Island. The tide was high and when she squinted she could see the rounded shapes of the golden harbor seals already sunning on the rocks. Better hurry if she was to get in her morning swim before breakfast.

She pulled on a bathing costume and grabbed a towel, creeping barefooted down the steep stairs. Everyone seemed to be asleep. Somehow she couldn't get used to the summer boarders her mother was taking in now that they'd moved from White Island to Haley's Island. Celia liked having her parents and younger brothers Oscar and Cedric to herself.

With care she closed the screen door and scrambled over the rocks to the pier, hoping her mother wasn't looking out the kitchen window. With Father away in Concord for his term in the New Hampshire House, Mother was twice as vigilant. Time and again she scolded Celia for going barefoot on the abrasive granite, constantly reminding her that it was time she behaved like a lady and not a mermaid.

Celia sat on an outcrop of rock near the pier and picked up a long strand of wild pink morning glories knotted around a piece of sea wrack. She looped it in a crown on her head, and selected another for a necklace.

The waves rippled gently over her toes and made a ruffle of foam soft as the fringe of an oyster. Across the channel Appledore Island blazed in the first rays of sun, and the mainland coastline glistened. It was one of those brilliant Shoals days when you could see clear to Cape Ann, Massachusetts, and as far north as Cape Elizabeth, Maine.

Attuned to the natural sounds around her, she started at the high warning shriek of a gull and the crunch of footsteps on jingle shells. Instinctively, she jumped up. Bother and tarnation. There was that Levi Thaxter fellow again. Ever since he'd arrived it had been Harvard this and Harvard that — not to mention that he'd taken over her room for the summer.

The best recourse was to pretend she hadn't seen him. With a burst of energy she sprang up and dove straight into the freezing water. Although it was mid-July, she had to keep every limb in motion so she wouldn't turn numb. Back and forth she swam, hoping he'd leave. Finally,when she saw that he hadn't budged, she swam back in.

"Water cold?" he asked as she clambered onto the beach.

"Not very," she answered, rubbing her thin arms briskly with the terry towel until the circulation returned.

He stroked his new beard. He'd started growing it that week and declared importantly that he'd never shave again as long as he was on the Shoals. It looked ridiculous. Wiry tufts of reddish hair sprouted here and there from his otherwise smooth angular chin. He stood on the rock outcrop above the inlet, a tall silhouette with folded arms.

She patted her braids dry, realizing to her dismay that she still was wearing the morning glory chain. How absurd she must look.

"Please don't take them off," the young man said in a pleading voice, blinking down at her. "You look like Queen Titania in *A Midsummer Night's Dream*."

Celia couldn't help hiding a smile behind her hand. She'd been told it was impolite, but what an extraordinary fellow he was. She'd just turned twelve and every time she looked at herself in the mirror she couldn't help wondering when her body would catch up to her mind.

Embarrassed by his presence, she bent to examine a flower growing near a small tidal pool. "Look, Mr. Thaxter. Do you know this flower? It's a scarlet pimpernel. Here on the Shoals we use it as a barometer. When it's going to storm, the petals close up tight."

Levi touched the flower with one long forefinger. "What a child of nature you are, Celia Laighton. Promise me you'll never grow up!" he said in an emotional outburst.

First a Shakespearean queen and now a child of nature. How silly mainlanders could be. She tossed the bedraggled flower garland onto the beach, grabbed her towel, and with as much dignity as she could muster, headed back toward the house. If Mother learned how petulantly she'd acted toward their guest, she'd have to apologize, but she simply couldn't take Mr. Thaxter's nonsense a minute longer.

Celia wasn't asked to give up her room a second summer. During the fall and spring her father and brothers transformed Haley's barn on Smutty-Nose Island into a separate inn they called The Mid-Ocean House — relying mostly on word of mouth among friends of the family to fill the rooms. To her consternation, Levi returned with his entire family. Later, his friends Thomas Higginson and John Weiss arrived. They both had finished their studies and were free-thinking ministers ready to take on the world and everyone with it.

Celia's father stayed on the Shoals to supervise. He entertained Franklin Pierce, a New Hampshire colleague who had been in the U.S. Senate, and Richard Dana, the popular author of *Two Years Before The Mast*.

One afternoon shortly after the inn opened, Celia cleared the dishes from the noon meal and wandered into the parlor. The kerosene lamps had been lit because of a sudden midday rainstorm. Mrs. Thaxter and her daughter Lucy were in the kitchen talking with Celia's mother. Her brothers Oscar and Cedric had gone into the cellar to the new bowling alley that occupied most of their waking hours.

She sat on the arm of her father's chair and affectionately stroked his shoulder while he talked.

"It's too early to spread the word, Thomas," Mr. Pierce said, "but between you and me, I've got my eye on the Presidential nomination. I hope you'll back me if I decide to run."

"I'll keep it under my hat, and I'm behind you all the way. But as for me, I'm making my fortune right here on the Isles, and the Mid-Ocean House is just the beginning."

"Nonsense, you come in with me," Pierce said. "We'll set up shop in Washington. You and Eliza can live in style, and Celia here will have her pick of the finest young men in the country."

He winked at Celia conspiratorially. But she knew her father all too well. He had no intention of leaving the Shoals — and neither had she. Besides, she wanted nothing to do with those snooty Washington lawyers and fusty old politicians. Levi Thaxter and his companion John Weiss would have to do. The two Harvard graduates were ensconced in a corner gesticulating and declaiming as though their very souls depended on it.

She excused herself, curled up on a windowseat, and stared pensively out at the rain. On White Island at least she'd been able to harbor her thoughts without constant confusion. Perhaps if she imagined the chatter came from a flock of squabbling sea gulls she could blend them into the background.

Thomas Higginson surprised her with his soft voice. "Mind if I intrude on your revery?"

She looked expectantly into his bright, clean-shaven face. They'd only just met, but she found him the most sympathetic of their guests so far.

"Your father tells me you were a great help to him when he was keeping the lighthouse on White Island," he said, sitting beside her.

Celia could feel her cheeks burn. She wasn't used to having others talk about her — or for that matter, to her. "I think he might have been humoring you, Mr. Higginson." She laughed nervously. "I was only a child. When I was older I did help Father trim the wicks on the red and gold lanterns, and we polished the copper reflectors together."

Higginson smiled kindly. "I imagine you kept each other company."

"That's it." Celia felt her shyness ebb as she talked. "When Father was away on the other islands, at dusk I'd take a lantern and wait near the boat slip to guide him in. The rocks on White Island are very treacherous."

He nodded gravely. "So you lived on one small acre for five whole years?" he asked in a tone of disbelief.

"It was smaller than an acre because half the island was taken up by the lighthouse and stone cottage. It was so small that our rain cistern, the whale oil tank, and a storage room for food all had to go underneath the tower."

He gave her a pitying look. "You must have been terribly lonely."

"Oh, not really," she objected. "My brothers and I explored every crevice and cranny, and I never was bored. The very first winter I woke up to a loud splintering noise. Mother's china was clattering in the cupboards, and then a wave broke my window and water came pouring onto the floor. I ran to Mother in the kitchen while Father and Ben pushed with all their might against the door to go save Betsy."

"The maid?"

"Heavens to Betsy," she said, and they both laughed. "She was our cow! We'd never think of abandoning her to the storm, so that night she stayed in the kitchen with us. In good weather I used to lead her across the pebbles to Seavey Island to graze. She always returned on her own before the tide came in."

"She was a smart cow." Higginson studied Celia's face. "What did you do after that?"

"We had no choice. We had to wait out the storm. Luckily, Father and Ben Whalen had already lighted the lamps in the tower and made it back to the house before the Trojan Horse was swept away by the waves. We were thankful the sailors could see the lights and wouldn't founder on the shoals."

Thoroughly engrossed, Thomas leaned closer to hear Celia over the downpour from a nearby gutter spout. "Forgive my ignorance, but what exactly do you mean by the Trojan Horse?"

She also leaned forward. "The covered catwalk to the lighthouse from the cottage. From a distance it always seemed like the Trojan Horse in Homer's *Iliad*."

"My, you're a well-educated young lady."

She smiled, pleased that at last someone realized she no longer was a child. "There's not much else to do out here in the wintertime but sit around the fire and read."

"And who's your favorite author?"

"Alfred Tennyson," she answered without hesitation.

"So you like poetry, do you?"

Celia had become strangely agitated by their conversation. "You ask a great deal of questions, Mr. Higginson," she objected, hoping to gain time to think his question through.

He scratched at a mosquito bite on his hand. "I guess it's the journalist in me. I'm a curious fellow, and you appear to have a natural ear for words. Maybe someday you'll write about your experiences on White Island."

Celia didn't know what to say. She pulled back the window curtain and pretended to look out. The people in this room had traveled and studied. They were orators like Levi or essayists like Mr. Higginson. Why, Mr. Pierce even was aspiring to be President. In the eight years she'd been on the Shoals she'd gone to the mainland only a few times, and then all she'd seen were Portsmouth dry goods stores!

Levi sauntered up and boomed for all the room to hear, "What's this *tête-à-tête* all about, Thomas? Getting sweet on Miss Laighton, are you?"

Mr. Higginson wasn't in a jesting mood. He glared at Levi. "I say, Thaxter, must you always act like you're on stage? Buzz off into the wings somewhere. Celia and I are talking."

Before they could go any further, Celia jumped up from the windowseat and stood between them. "The rain's letting up," she interjected. "I think I'll walk out to Haley's sea wall. Does anyone want to come along?"

The ledges were slippery from the rain. Celia led the way with Levi and John Weiss staggering as they braced themselves against the stiff breeze and sang Harvard songs at the top of their lungs. Her eight-year-old brother Cedric made uninvited wisecracks and tagged along behind Levi's sister and Thomas Higginson.

Lucy stopped to tighten a lace on her high-button shoe, giving Thomas a chance to ply Celia with still more questions. "What's behind the name Smutty-Nose?"

Celia hung over the pathway and watched the whitecaps break and fan along the steep coast. "There's something sinister about that name. I like to think of it as Haley's Island. Anyway, at the other end there's a promontory of dangerous black rocks that have caused several shipwrecks. So the sailors named it after the smutch of rocks on the hook-nosed point."

"You mean booger!" Cedric shouted, squeezing among them. Higginson tousled his hair while Celia glared at her brother.

Lucy placed her hands over her ears. "I'm not sure what's worse, the tumult of the waves and wind or my brother's so-called singing."

Celia laughed. Thomas offered his arm to each of them and beamed. "Ah, smell that fresh ocean breeze." He inhaled deeply.

John turned and faced them. "Levi and I have had a disagreement, Celia. I say the Isles of Shoals number seven. I even counted them for him, but he still insists there are nine. Who's right?"

"Both of you."

"But, I say, how can that be?"

Cedric came running up and plowed into Celia's skirts. "Cedie, do behave," she pleaded. "Answer Mr. Weiss or I'll box your ears off."

Her brother squirmed in her arms as she held him fast. "At high tide there are nine islands, Mr. Weiss," Cedric said, and he recited them, screwing up his face and counting on his fingers. "Seavey and White, Smutty-Nose and Malaga, Cedar, Star, Appledore, Duck and Londoner."

"And at low tide?" she prodded.

"Malaga's connected to Smutty-Nose and Seavey to White Island. So they pop up." He hesitated and then added, "Like me!" Rushing from Celia's arms, he ducked beneath the path onto the slippery rocks below.

Levi shouted after him, "Cedric, get back to your sister this instant." Surprised by his concern and control over the situation, Celia waved her thanks. Perhaps she had been too hard on Mr. Thaxter.

As soon as they reached the sea wall, Cedric climbed to the top of one of the giant granite boulders and waved his arms frantically. "Friends, Romans, Countrymen, lend me your ears," he shouted. When nobody paid any attention, he screamed, "Listen! Listen!"

Celia tapped her foot impatiently and with her hands on her hips she ordered, "Get down right now."

With a downcast face the little boy sat dejectedly on the rock. "I just wanted to tell them about Captain Haley and the wall he built."

"Oh, all right," she said. "But promise me that after you've told them you won't bother us anymore."

Now that he'd been granted permission, Cedric hemmed and hawed. "Well, you see, Samuel Haley was really a good man. He lighted a candle in the window of his house every night and had a cot made up so that if any sailor strayed ashore..."

"Get on with it," Celia interrupted. "You were going to tell them about the sea wall."

"Anyway, Mr. Haley was down here by the shore and he happened to turn over a flat rock and found four bars of silver that pirates had left on the island.."

John Weiss let out a long low whistle.

Bolstered by the attention, Cedric continued. "So he took the bars of silver and exchanged them for enough money to build the sea wall."

"Now, Cedric, you aren't putting us on, are you?" Thomas asked.

Celia cut in. "Oh, no, Mr. Higginson, every word that Cedric says is absolutely true. This wall was built with pirate silver."

They all clapped and cheered as her brother hopped down from his makeshift podium. When he was out of earshot, Levi commented, "That boy has a bit of ham in him."

"You should know, Levi," Thomas said.

This time Levi just shrugged it off and leapt onto the boulder Cedric had vacated. "From ham to Hamlet," he announced.

With a tremendously powerful voice that resonated over the crashing waves, Levi Thaxter hypnotized them with Hamlet's solioquy. His gestures were few, and the power of the performance came from the modulation of his voice. Celia's heart beat as fast as her hands while she joined the others with bravos and claps of admiration. None of them moved, waiting for an encore.

"Go on," Lucy begged, her face filled with pride at her older brother's obvious talent.

Levi shook his head and stroked his wiry beard as he stared down at them. Then, unexpectedly, he vaulted from the rock and stood before Celia. He took her hand and led her onto the rock, jumped back down and looked up at her.

Celia pulled down the brim of her sun bonnet, attempting to hide behind it. Unlike her brother Cedric, she didn't enjoy being the center of attention. But in an instant she realized their eyes once more were glued on Levi and his passionate dramatic sketch.

> *But soft! What light through yonder window breaks?*
> *It is the east, and Juliet is the sun!*
> *Arise, fair sun, and kill the envious moon,*
> *Who is already sick and pale with grief.*

All of a sudden Cedric's head popped up just behind Celia. He rolled his eyes comically to the sky, and with his hands over his heart in a high shrill voice he cried, "Oh Romeo, Romeo! Wherefore art thou Romeo?"

Celia whirled around. She stamped her foot and grabbed for her brother. They all laughed. Then she laughed too, although she was boiling mad.

The spell broken, Levi walked up to her, put his long firm fingers around Celia's waist, and lifted her down. Thunder rumbled in the distance and the sun once more had disappeared behind dark thunderheads.

"We should be getting back," Celia warned. They let her shepherd them up the incline and onto the boardwalk.

Levi strode beside her as they hurried toward the inn. "Don't be angry at Cedric," he said after a long silence. "Your brother's jealous because you've grown up and are leaving him behind."

Celia stared into his dark eyes. Her heart started racing again. "Well, he has no earthly reason to be jealous," she said, pretending to be cross.

"Oh, yes, he does." Levi slipped his arm around her waist. "Because I'm the one who will be with you the rest of the summer."

2

Cedric waited at the door to Celia's bedroom while she fastened the top seashell button on her dress. She rushed after him toward the parlor where Oscar already was conjugating Latin verbs at the round oak table. She flashed her new tutor what she hoped was a convincing smile. "Sorry, I'm a little late. I still haven't unpacked yet."

Levi Thaxter jumped to his feet and pulled out a chair for her. The boys exchanged looks of exasperation. It was bad enough that they had to listen to their father extolling Mr. Thaxter, Sr., night and day for his help in buying Appledore Island and the new hotel. But now they had to sit and watch their own sister turn into a dumbstruck nitwit every time she was in the same room with Levi Thaxter, Jr.

They studied between noisy interruptions by the workmen sawing and hammering so the Appledore House would be completed by the June fifteenth grand opening. When Levi no longer could hear his students over the racket, he dismissed them. Celia reluctantly picked up her books. Her brothers, glad to play hooky for the day, were out the door like a shot, but she idled at the table, glancing under her long lashes at Levi, and asking him about a problem which she'd solved ages ago.

The persistent hammering drowned out his answer. "Bring along your books," he shouted, "and we'll get away from this din."

They left the Laighton cottage and turned toward a wide cove of sandy beach. A flock of sandpipers flew off the water and landed in front of them. The tiny birds flitted a few paces ahead, their sharp beaks in constant motion as they pecked at the wet sand for beach fleas and skeleton shrimp.

Celia sashayed in and out, playing tag with the waves. Levi strolled over to an oasis of beach roses and spread his jacket in the shade against some low polished stones. A song sparrow perched on a twig and sang a high clear aria. "He's looking for a mate," she said.

"Let's hope the poor fellow doesn't have to wait long," Levi said and motioned for her to sit with him. She settled in the shade and opened a math book. But, as she'd hoped, Levi stopped her. "Your tutor's got a bad case of spring fever." He sighed. "I'm afraid you'll have to indulge him."

"So have I," she admitted. "It's so beautiful today."

He leaned on one elbow and with the other he swept the dry sand between them, exposing a damp patch beneath. "Here's a problem for you, Miss Laighton."

"But I thought you said we weren't going to study."

"I think you will be able to solve this equation without too much trouble." He turned, picked up a dry twig from underneath a rose bush, and drew a large lopsided heart in the sand, placing his initials in the top half.

She looked down at the heart, looked out to sea, looked everywhere except at Levi. Was this a game he was playing to tease her or did he really mean it? She took the twig from his hand, and in big bold capitals she wrote her initials beneath his.

He tilted her chin upward and leaned over to kiss her. She wasn't surprised. All last summer he'd stolen kisses, but since her father had hired him to teach them, he'd kept a careful distance. "I love you, Celia," he said, retracing the letters. "I want to marry you."

All winter long she'd thought about Levi and longed to see him. You're going to be only fourteen and he's already twenty-five, she argued with herself. And yet, when she was with him nothing else seemed to matter.

Her mother had guessed right away. One snowy day when Celia was particularly restless, they talked about Levi. "Don't be in such a hurry," Eliza Laighton warned her daughter. "There are plenty of other fish in the sea." She dearly loved her mother, but this time she didn't understand. Celia didn't want anyone else. She wanted Levi.

Mistaking silence for rejection, Levi had smoothed over the heart with the palm of his hand. The song sparrow wove a figure eight against the radiant sky and returned to the same branch, repeating its clear searching song.

"There's a woman," Levi whispered, staring ahead at the sparkling waves.

Celia felt as though her entire life were hanging in the balance. Her parents always had made decisions for her and now she was being asked to abandon them and follow this man beside her.

"There's a woman—" he repeated louder, taking her hand in his. "She says *'My days were sunless and my nights were moonless— Parched the pleasant April herbage, and the lark's heart's outbreak tuneless, if you loved me not!'*"

He paused, twisting the top shell button of her dress between the fingers of his other hand. " *'And I who adore her'* " he slid the shell out of the buttonhole—" *' Who am mad to lay my spirit prostrate palpably before her—'* " He undid the next button.

Celia held her breath, letting the excitement of what he was doing pulse through her body.

" *'I may enter at her portal soon, as now her lattice takes me.'* " His hand slipped beneath the cloth onto her bare skin. " *'And by noontide as by midnight make her mine, as hers she makes me.'* " With the last word he pressed his lips to hers, pinning one arm to her side and gently forcing her flat onto the sand. At first she kissed him back, but when his hand stole beneath her camisole, she grabbed his wrist.

He persisted, holding her against him while he explored with his fingers, his face flushed and his tongue in her mouth. She twisted back and forth and, with a strong lunge, rolled away from him. It was a movement she'd invented to escape her brothers when they ganged up on her.

Without a word Levi brushed the sand off his shirt, stood up, and stalked toward the ocean.

Confused by remorse and guilt, she buttoned her dress and smoothed back her hair, so overcome with emotion she couldn't think. Was it her fault? Should she have given in?

"Levi?"

When he didn't answer or turn around, she brushed the sand from her dress and slowly walked up to him, still unsure of what she would say.

"Levi?" she repeated, standing in front of him so he had to look at her. "I'll be your fiancé." The surprise of what she'd said echoed inside her.

All the way back they stopped to gaze at each other and twirl around in each others' arms. Celia made Levi promise not to break the news of their engagement until after the hotel opened, knowing that her father's consent depended on the success of his business venture. When they were in sight of the Laighton cottage, they let go of each other's hands. At the last moment Levi pulled her behind the wall of an outlying tool shed. "Just one more kiss, then I'll leave."

Her face still smarted from his thick beard and she shook her head vehemently even while giving in to the frenzy of his caresses. At the sound of her father's voice Celia cried out in alarm. Levi groaned, letting his arms drop to the side.

"So this is what I've been paying you to teach my daughter!" Thomas Laighton wasn't an imposing man, but what he lacked in physical stature was heightened by the calm resolve and character in his face. The weathered endurance of island living combined with the proud bearing of public office presented a formidable obstacle to the young lovers.

"Mr. Laighton, Sir, it isn't what it seems," Levi objected.

"Levi, not now," Celia whispered, backing against the shed wall.

"Oh, it isn't?" her father asked. He smiled faintly. "It seems to me that you were kissing my daughter and she was kissing you back."

Levi stepped forward. "But you see, Sir—."

"Not now, Levi," Celia warned him again, louder.

"Yes, Levi, she's right. I've got work to do and so do you. As long as you're working for me, you'll do as I say and stay away from my daughter. Is that clear?"

Levi looked tenderly down at Celia and then at her father. "Mr. Laighton, I want to marry her."

She had never in her life felt as if she was going to faint, but decided this might be as good a time as any. She braced herself against the tool shed while her father stood before them in silence, his lips firmly clamped together. She closed her eyes. When she opened them, her father's face was livid.

"Get off this island and stay off!" he commanded, the order all the more dreadful because he didn't raise his voice. "The steamer's bringing in a load of lumber this afternoon and I want you to be on it when it goes back. I'll tell your father."

Celia threw her arms around her father's neck. "Please don't send him away," she implored. "Father, please."

"I thought I'd raised a daughter with some sense," he said, pushing her away.

"But Levi and I are in love." Tears spilled down her cheeks.

"That's ridiculous. He's old enough to know better, even if you don't. It's robbing the cradle."

"But Mr. Laighton—."

Thomas Laighton took Levi aside. "Come now, son. Do as I say. Celia's still a child. She's never really known anyone but her own family. This is just a school girl's infatuation. My daughter needs time to grow up, and if you love her you'll give her that chance."

For weeks Celia wouldn't talk to her father unless spoken to. Her mother tried to patch things up between them, but her distraught daughter kept a polite distance, doing only what her father asked, and nothing more.

One August evening she sat on a rocker on the cottage piazza and watched the stars appear one by one. Soon the sky was a kaleidoscope of constellations over the dark islands. To the south— the three stars in Orion's belt, and higher, her favorite little sisters, the Pleiades. She'd just learned a poem about them: *"The moon has set, and the Pleiades. It is the middle of the night. Time passes. And I lie alone."* Although it had been written almost two thousand years before, it matched her own feelings so perfectly that Celia felt as if she knew the Greek woman who wrote it.

The rocker beside hers creaked, and her father sat down. He rocked back and forth, the smoke from his pipe drifting upward. She gripped the arms of her chair, prepared for the awkward silence that had grown up between them.

A star shot in an arc through the Milky Way, then another. Star showers were like migrating whales, always touching off an inexplicable excitement deep inside her.

"Did you wish for Levi on that star?" her father asked, his face hidden by the wicker chair frame.

She sighed. "If you really want to know, Father, I wished we could be friends. I'm so tired of being angry at you."

He stopped rocking. "I've missed you too, Celie. Come on over here and talk to me."

She pulled her rocker over so the arm rests were touching and held out her hand. "Truce?"

Her father placed his rough palm over hers. "Yes, my darling daughter. Truce. You know we love you. Your mother and I have been worried sick that we haven't prepared you for the real world."

"The Shoals are the—."

He patted her hand. "Hear me out, dear. Life on the Shoals is wonderful and I wouldn't trade it for anything. But one has to know the world first in order to renounce it."

Celia watched a star shower cascade over the black expanse of water. It was breathtakingly beautiful. Yet...until she'd met Levi she'd been completely contented with her life on the islands. But somehow he'd filled her with desires, and now she had an insatiable appetite to see, do, and be everything.

Her father pushed a hand through his greying hair. "Your mother and I think we've come up with a solution for your ultimate happiness."

Celia sat on the edge of her chair waiting for him to tell her she could marry Levi after all.

He spread his short fingers on his knees. "We've decided to send you away to school."

Stunned, she dropped back against the chair cushion.

Despite her obvious disappointment her father continued talking about how the Mt. Washington Seminary was the best girls' school in Boston. Mr. Thaxter had highly recommended it, and even suggested that she could room with his daughter Lucy.

At the mention of her best friend and Levi's sister, Celia perked up considerably. Could her parents be on her side after all?

Thomas Laighton smiled at his daughter's sudden interest. "Levi will be working for his father at the law office so you won't be seeing much of him, but—."

"Oh, Father, thank you. Thank you!" She jumped up and kissed him on the cheek.

"Don't thank me. Thank your mother." He smiled from ear to ear. "Eliza convinced me we've kept you too isolated out here."

With uncontrolled gaiety Celia skipped halfway down the piazza and back.

"Now mind you, young lady, this doesn't mean we've changed our minds about you and Levi. We both think you're much too young for marriage."

"Yes, Father," she agreed obediently.

"We're paying an arm and a leg for your room and board so we expect you to study hard, and abide by the rules."

"Oh, yes, Father, I will." Celia collapsed back into the rocker and waited for another falling star to wish on.

Were it not for the possibility of seeing Levi, Celia would have returned to the Shoals in less than a month. She liked her classes, and the girls were all right, but she missed the salt air and the sound of the ocean. For ten years she'd lived near the water, and now she realized how much the Atlantic had become part of her. Several times a day she walked outside to look at the sky.

"You're beginning to sound newspaperial," Lucy joked one day as Celia stuck her head out the window for the third time, and announced there was a wind from the northeast with snow likely.

Celia's mother had packed three dresses, which Celia considered two too many. However, most of the girls were from wealthy Bostonian families and recently had "come out." Their favorite topic centered on what they had worn, or would wear, to younger friends' coming out parties. Celia had never seen so many costly, high-fashion bustles, gowns, and satin slippers.

When she turned up at the bimonthly *thé dansant* in her grey muslin with the seashell buttons, she overheard one girl remark, "Will you look at the dull dress Celia Laighton has on?" Fortunately, before she could give the comment a second thought, she was accosted by a pimply-faced boy asking her to dance. With serious concentration he stepped on her toes and twice managed to kick her ankles.

"Thank you," she told him when he tagged behind her like a lost puppy, "I think I'll sit the next one out."

Lucy also had abandoned her partner and joined Celia on the chairs lined against the wall. "This is truly dreadful," she whispered. "Was yours as bad as mine?"

"They should call this horrid dance the *thé grincent*," Celia quipped, easing her sore toes out of her slippers.

"You're right. It's enough to put anyone's teeth on edge," Lucy agreed, laughing aloud. The dance instructor looked disapprovingly their way. "I'm already scheming how we can get out of the next one," she added.

"Good, because my poor feet won't survive many more assaults by these clod-hopping prep school Lotharios," Celia said, noting that the instructor was moving toward them with two more gawky boys on each arm.

Lucy sighed. "I'll tell you my plan later."

Celia could endure anything as long as she would be seeing Levi soon. "Does it involve your brother?"

"Of course, you ninny. Father's been keeping him under tight reins. But," she whispered, "there are big plans underfoot for the holidays."

The instructor had deposited the two boys, and a short plump specimen with red cheeks and freckles bowed to Celia. "May I have this dance?"

She gave him her most radiant smile. "Why, of course, you may. I'd be enchanted," she said, taking his clammy hand in hers. She cast a backward glance at Lucy, who was being swept off the floor by an energetic, four-foot midget with Brilliantined hair.

Mrs. Thaxter met the two school girls at the door and had Lucy usher Celia upstairs to a room on the third floor, apologizing that it was in the maids' quarters, but she thought Celia might like to have a room of her own. Obviously, her real motive was to keep Celia and Levi a floor apart.

The Watertown house was unlike anything Celia had ever seen. It was richly elegant with dark mahogany paneling, leaded glass windows, and exquisite heirloom furniture. As she sat in the parlor helping Lucy string popcorn and cranberries for the Christmas tree, she looked around at the ornate gilt-framed mirrors, huge oil paintings, and fine Persian carpets. How different they were from the worn rockers and rag carpets she'd grown up with.

Seeing the tall spruce tree indoors also seemed magically strange to Celia. Her mother always prepared a special dinner on Christmas day, but her parents never had bothered much with decorations since the Isles had no evergreens. Well, there had been some scrawny dwarfed cedar trees on Cedar Island, but they were stunted beyond recognition.

She and Lucy draped their garlands around the tree and stood back to admire their work. "Oh, it's lovely!" Celia exclaimed.

"Wait!" Lucy took a box from under the tree and removed several dozen small candle holders. "We'll fasten these to the branches and light them tonight after we return from church."

Levi didn't appear until Mr. Thaxter came home with his son at suppertime. Celia greeted Levi eagerly, but they had little opportunity to talk before Mrs. Thaxter hurried them out the door to the Christmas Eve service.

The church sanctuary was even more imposing than the house, with a wide aisle that seemed to take forever to walk down. Dressed in elegant fur and velvet finery, Mr. and Mrs. Thaxter let the two girls enter the pew first, leaving Levi on the far side of them. As the organ resounded through the vaulted transept with all stops pulled for "Joy to the World," Celia brushed a tear from her cheek, overcome by a wave of homesickness.

Christmas day she ran to the window of her bedroom. Big white flakes drifted onto the rooftops and blanketed the large sugar maples that lined the alley to the carriage shed. She poured water into a porcelain bowl, scooped it into her hands, and dipped her face, patting it dry with the finely embroidered towel that had been set out for her. She was braiding her hair when Lucy knocked, excited as a young child and anxious to get downstairs to open her presents.

Levi was waiting on the landing, and he grabbed her hand. Lucy tittered, looking around to see if her parents were in sight. "The coast is clear," she whispered.

"In that case —." Levi pulled Celia toward him, boldly kissing her on the mouth. "Merry Christmas, dearest Celia."

Before she had time to respond in kind, Mr. Thaxter's voice boomed up the stairs. "No presents until you've had your breakfast," he ordered sternly. "So you'd better get down here."

She opened the parcel her family had sent and exchanged gifts with Lucy. Levi had bought his mother a silk Florentine scarf which she proudly tossed around her neck. When Celia was given a similar box with a scarf of a different color, Mrs. Thaxter smiled coldly at her. "How nice of my son to think of you, Miss Laighton," she said in a monotone.

Dinner was interminable, the Thaxters being extremely formal. Celia sat quietly next to Lucy trying to emulate every move so she wouldn't use the wrong utensil or drink from the wrong glass. Levi ate heartily, and flashed sympathetic looks at her across the table while his family talked pleasantries.

In the late afternoon, after they'd all retired for a nap, Levi came into the parlor. He was wearing his overcoat and had flung Celia's hooded cape over his arm. "We're going for a short stroll," he said.

Mr. Thaxter looked up from a book. "What's that?"

Lucy shoved Celia forward. "Hurry," she whispered. "Before Mother gets back from the kitchen!"

Mr. Thaxter glanced up again, but before he could say anything, Levi had her halfway out the front door.

The snow had dusted glare ice on the walkway and Celia nearly slipped rushing down the steps. Levi caught her, and they crossed arms, sliding along like skaters and laughing at the success of their escape.

"I have so much to tell you," he said, stopping to catch his breath.

"And I you. I thought I'd never see you again."

"My parents seemed even more upset with our marriage plans than yours. Father insisted that I go to work for him and I hate it." Levi glowered. "When we're married, Celia, I swear I won't practice law."

"But Levi, what will we live on?" At once she regretted the question.

"I can always act, or teach. I'm a good tutor."

"Oh, yes, you are!" she agreed. "You are talented, Levi, and I think you could have a wonderful career as an actor."

He smiled down at her. "Dearest Celia, you make a fellow feel special."

She pulled up her hood, and they walked briskly as he continued.

"Do you remember the poem I recited to you that day on the beach?"

How could she forget? Every moment of that day sparkled in her memory.

"Well, a British poet named Robert Browning wrote it, and I've been corresponding with him. Mr. Longfellow has asked me to read some of Browning's poems at the Saturday Literary Club."

"You actually know the author of *'Evangeline?'*" Celia asked with excitement. She had just read the book-length poem in her English class.

"Henry's a good friend," he said nonchalantly. "I met him when I was at Harvard. Anyway, it's a great honor to be asked to read."

"Oh, may I come?" She clutched his arm and pulled it as if to yank an invitation out of him.

He smiled at her childish naiveté. "I'm afraid women aren't allowed."

"And why not?" She folded her arms across her chest in annoyance. "Aren't women interested in poetry, too?"

"Of course. I didn't know you were interested in women's suffrage," he said, humoring her.

Celia's voice lost some of its bravado. "What do you mean?"

"One woman, one vote, and all that." This determined independence was what he liked most about her. "If you really want to hear me, I'll have Henry invite you and some other friends to his home in Cambridge for a private reading. How's that?"

"Would you do that just for me?" She looked up at him with admiration.

"Of course, dear heart."

They strolled along the sycamore-lined avenue past houses that seemed to Celia as grand as hotels. A pair of boys ran from the circular drive to one of the mansions and bombarded them with snowballs. Levi ducked and Celia whirled around, the snow exploding on her neck. Laughing, she ran into the snow and sent a volley of snowballs back at the retreating youngsters.

Levi watched with bewilderment. Young ladies of his acquaintance were not in the habit of engaging in snowball fights. Celia's cheeks were rosy as he picked her up in his arms, placed her solidly on the cleared path, and paternally brushed the snow from the hem of her skirt with the backs of his gloves.

"Lucy has told me about your Friday tea dances," he resumed.

"Couldn't we talk of something else?" she asked, slipping her arm comfortably through his. "I can't stand those to-dos."

"We have to be getting back," he said with a worried look. "My parents are worse than the Montagues, and this is important. I don't know when we'll have another chance to talk. The day of your next dance, Lucy will report to the head mistress that you're ill, persuading her that you'd be better off here with us in Watertown."

She smiled with tenderness, realizing that Levi would be risking his father's ire.

"Besides," he added, "I won't have you dancing with strangers."

She squeezed his arm playfully. "Why, Levi Thaxter, I believe you're jealous."

He pretended not to hear. "The following dance, Lucy will come down with the grippe, and this time you'll bring her home. After that, we'll have to devise a new strategy."

That evening as she lay in bed Celia savored every detail of the day, culminating with the sweet closeness between them as they'd walked and talked. Only last night she'd desperately longed for home. Tonight she longed for Levi.

The day after Christmas Mr. Thaxter dragged his son back to the law offices. The entire week Celia and Lucy played endless games of Parchisi and waited impatiently for New Year's eve when they were invited to a grand ball in Boston.

The afternoon of what Lucy called "the social event of the year," she urged Celia to try on one of her elaborate ball gowns.

To please her, Celia slipped a burgundy gown with black lace trim, pleats, and ruffles over her head, and laughed at herself in the mirror.

"It's very becoming," Lucy said, fastening a hook and eye at the neck. "Please wear it."

"But it doesn't feel like me," Celia complained. "I couldn't spend an entire evening in this. I want to be comfortable so I can concentrate on what's going on around me." Aware that she might have hurt Lucy's feelings, she took out the barrette her friend had given her for Christmas. "Look, this will dress me up a bit."

Lucy hugged her. "We're so different, but I love you like a sister."

"Sister-in-law?" Celia asked the dark-haired girl in gold taffeta.

"Oh, yes, I can hardly wait until you're a member of the family."

"Nor can I."

As the girls came down the stairs, Mrs. Thaxter cast a look of dismay at Celia's plain ivory satin gown.

Noting the woman's disapproval, Celia self-consciously focused on a stair tread and fiddled with a seashell bracelet she was wearing. She brightened when Levi appeared and made up for his mother's reserve with effusive compliments. "You girls —." He cleared his throat. "I mean, you women look like something right out of Botticelli."

"I wonder if Botticelli's muses had to wear corsets," Lucy bantered.

"As I remember," Mr. Thaxter said, entering the hall, "one of them wore nothing." The comment seemed so uncharacteristic that Celia couldn't help laughing.

Mrs. Thaxter shook her head disparagingly. "That will do."

With a flourish, Mr. Thaxter doffed his top hat at the girls on the stairs. "My son is absolutely right. You both look lovely as a picture."

It was the first time he had shown any kindness at all to Celia, and she smiled at him with gratitude.

The gala affair was held in a private mansion with a marble foyer and indoor fountain circled with poinsettias. Their wraps were taken, and Levi and the two girls were ushered upstairs to the mirrored ballroom where only a handful of young people danced beneath garlands of greenery criss-crossing the muraled ceiling of the great hall. A fire crackled in a gigantic grate at the far end.

No sooner had they settled into the crowd milling on the periphery of the room than Levi was greeted by a congenial man who pumped his hand and eyed Celia with unabashed curiosity. "Ah, is this a particular friend of your sister's, or yours?" the white-haired gentleman asked pointedly.

"Mine," Lucy and Levi answered in unison and smiled at each other.

Levi stepped forward. "Celia Laighton, may I present Henry Wadsworth Longfellow, friend and mentor." In a teasing tone, he added, "And the celebrated author of *Evangeline*."

"Oh, Mr. Longfellow!" Celia completely lost her composure when she realized she was meeting the great poet. At a loss for words, she extended her hand. But when the distinguished writer bent to kiss it, her seashell bracelet slipped down and his lips landed instead on the fluted pink shells.

"And what have we here?" he asked with a surprised look.

"Oh dear, I'm sorry," she apologized, embarrassed, pushing the bracelet back onto her arm. "It's a memento from the Isles of Shoals."

He winked at her. "Aha! Just as I thought. Levi has gone and affianced himself to a sea sprite."

Celia blushed, looking toward Levi to counter Mr. Longfellow's jests. But Thomas Higginson and John Weiss had come up, and suddenly she was surrounded with handsome young men in black ties and tails.

"How charming you look this evening, Celia," Thomas said. "How are you getting on?"

"Like a flower near a beehive," Longfellow interjected and chuckled. Then he turned to converse with a couple behind him,.

Higginson whisked Celia onto the dance floor before Levi could object. He was an extremely competent dancer and she floated around the room, enjoying the lilt of the music and the whirl of colors as they wove in and out among the other couples.

When the dance was over, she returned to Levi, who again was talking with Mr. Longfellow and a shortish older woman while gesturing with animation. "And I'll be reading his poems," he was saying.

"I know the Brownings. Met them in Italy," the woman stated flatly.

"You do?" Levi's eyes lighted up as though he was seeing her for the first time.

"Yes, and I much prefer Elizabeth's sonnets to Robert's work. But then, I'm not a poet." The woman looked at Celia with Levi on one side of her and Thomas on the other. "Who's this beauty?"

"Mrs. Stowe, may I introduce you to Celia Laighton," Mr. Longfellow said. "And, Celia, this is Harriet Beecher Stowe, author of the serialized stories called *Uncle Tom's Cabin* which have been keeping my wife and me up until midnight every night."

Celia hadn't heard of the woman, but she wondered what Mrs. Thaxter would have thought of Mrs. Stowe's common black dress without any adornment or jewelry of any kind.

"Now, Henry, don't go blaming your insomnia on me," the woman retorted, staring at Celia. "What do you do, my dear?"

Celia had never been asked the question before and it startled her. "I'm going to the Mt. Washington Seminary," she said.

Mrs. Stowe stepped closer. "I can tell you aren't from Boston. Not that it's a sin, you understand."

"I'm from the Isles of Shoals," Celia said. "It's a group of islands off the coast at Portsmouth. But, of course, you already know that," she added quickly.

Mrs. Stowe nodded. "I've seen them on my way up to Maine. Always wondered who lived way out there. They remind me of the White Cliffs of Dover over in England the way they stand out above the water." She ruminated aloud as though no one were listening to her. "Be a good place to hide something — or someone."

Celia was wondering if she should tell Mrs. Stowe about the bars of silver when the strange woman blurted out, "Slaves!"

"I beg your pardon?"

"Do you have any slaves on those islands of yours?"

Was the woman out of her mind? Why would there be slaves on Appledore? "When Mother puts me to work in the kitchen at the Appledore Hotel, I often feel like a slave," Celia answered somewhat flippantly.

The plump plain woman smiled, and when she did suddenly her face was radiant. "I like this girl," she said to no one in particular. "And you say your father owns a hotel?"

"Yes, but before that he was a lighthouse keeper."

"Goodness gracious. What an interesting family. And is he an abolitionist?"

Celia looked up at Levi for support, but he and Longfellow were talking. "Father's a politician."

Mrs. Stowe laughed so loudly that people nearby turned to see what was going on. "Well, my dear, that's close enough for me. Don't worry, though. I promise not to bore you with my ideas on slavery." She took Celia by the elbow. "When I asked you what you do, I thought an independent soul like you might have grand plans for the future."

Celia glanced shyly at Levi. "We're going to be married," she said, hoping Levi didn't mind. After all, he had told Henry Longfellow so it wasn't exactly a secret. Besides, she decidedly liked Mrs. Stowe's forthright manner. "Levi's father and mine built the hotel together."

Mrs. Stowe frowned. "Aha. So that explains it. But dear, aren't you too young to marry?" she asked bluntly.

The dowdy woman focused all of her energy on Celia, seeming to dredge up deep-seated feelings and doubts about her marriage which she thought had been settled. Mrs. Stowe had the same uncanny penchant as her mother for getting to the heart of the matter.

The matronish woman patted Celia's arm affectionately. "Don't worry. Everything that ought to happen is going to happen," she said.

Celia didn't know whether to laugh or wonder at the wisdom of the remark.

"Well, I should be getting back." Mrs. Stowe yawned. "Before I go, though, I want an invitation to that Appledore Hotel of yours. I'll need some rest after the publication of my book."

"We'd love to have you," Celia offered, shaking her hand vigorously. Mr. Longfellow was brusquely interrupted to see

Mrs. Stowe to the cloakroom, and for the first time that evening Celia and Levi were left alone.

The new year flew by with one reception, reading, and dinner party after another until it was time for Celia to pack and return to the Shoals. Her father wrote that he knew she was continuing to see Levi. Since the match seemed inevitable, he'd rehired him to tutor the boys, and Levi would stay at the Thaxter cottage.

That summer the hotel filled quickly, and to escape the constant hustle and bustle, Celia retreated to the far end of the island to be with her fiancé.

One morning she returned to her room and found the maid still tidying up. Bubbling over with excitement, Celia chatted familiarly with the Norwegian fisherman's wife who came from Smutty-Nose to clean the Laighton cottage. "I'm getting married," she announced proudly.

The woman smiled. "I see little Celia with tall man has beard."

"That's Levi." Celia gazed at herself in the mirror. "I'm going to be Mrs. Thaxter."

The small dark woman momentarily stopped smoothing the bedspread. "Th - ax - ter," she repeated in broken English. "Is a strange name," she added.

Celia laughed. "And what's so strange about it?"

The maid stood behind her in the mirror. "Because it have axe in the middle," she said, crossing herself.

Celia turned around. "Nonsense. Next you'll be telling me I'm a seal because my name's Celia. What a queer thing to say."

The maid plumped a pillow for good measure and left. Celia sat down at a small table near the window. She wrote Levi's name on a sheet of paper. After staring at it for several minutes, she took her Bible from the bedside table and turned to *Leviticus VI*, reading a verse at random: "When there is sprinkled blood upon any garment, thou shalt wash it in a holy place."

With a decisive smack she closed the Bible and crumpled the paper in her hand. She didn't need a Bible to know that if they weren't married soon the only sin Levi would have to worry about would be fornication.

3

Celia and Levi were married the last day of September. On the morning of the wedding Celia took a walk over the clear, frost-covered island and gathered armfuls of goldenrod, asters, and bright maroon huckleberry branches for the parlor. Levi sailed to Portsmouth to fetch a minister, and Celia's mother supervised the baking of a wedding cake with White Mountain frosting.

The newlyweds stayed on Appledore for their honeymoon, then went to Watertown to live with Levi's family. In early December Celia discovered she was pregnant. Levi wasn't working yet, and concern showed on his face when she told him. "Don't worry," she said, "our families will stand by us." But the Thaxters' reception of the news was less than enthusiastic. "That was fast," Mrs. Thaxter said, raising an eyebrow. "When is the baby due, in April?"

With a look that could kill, Levi turned away from his mother and took his young bride in his arms. But it was too late. Her insinuating remark cut Celia to the quick, and as soon as weather permitted, they took the pack boat back to Appledore.

Karl was the first baby born on the Isles in a century, and everyone made a great fuss over him. Her mother sewed an entire wardrobe of blankets, smocks, and bonnets, and her father bounced the baby on his knee so vigorously she had to rescue the little tyke. Levi read him poetry until his newborn son fell asleep from sheer boredom. Even her brothers couldn't leave Karl alone. They goo-gooed and grinned or pulled his tiny toes and fingers trying to get him to smile. But most of the time the baby either gazed absently at the ceiling or cried until his face turned a startling reddish purple.

One afternoon after she'd put the baby down for his nap, Levi returned to the cottage with a guest from the hotel. The young man was writing a biography of Franklin Pierce, who already was on the Presidential campaign trail. Franklin, their mutual friend, summered on Appledore, and had sent Nathaniel Hawthorne in his stead, suggesting the Isles would make a good place to write.

"Mr. Pierce frequently talks about the Isles of Shoals," the quiet young man told them. "He regrets not being here."

"So are you going to put us in your book?" Levi winked at Celia as though he were joking, but she suspected he wouldn't mind a footnote or two for posterity.

Mr. Hawthorne sat timidly looking at his folded hands, occasionally stealing a glance around the room. He doesn't miss a thing, Celia thought, regretting the cracked plaster walls. She'd tried to cover them over with her own watercolor paintings and prints by some Italian Masters she'd cut from a magazine. But the cracks still spread like spider webs over the ceiling. She smoothed wisps of hair from her forehead and smiled at the introspective young author.

"Do you know who this is?" Levi asked in high-pitched excitement, not realizing he was putting her on the spot. Celia hadn't read anything but newspapers since the baby was born.

She paused, then ventured, "He's a talented author who at this very moment would rather be sitting at his desk working on his new book than listening to our praises of his last one."

The corners of Hawthorne's lips turned up and he leaned forward ever so slightly. "Your wife is perceptive, Mr. Thaxter," he said softly, "and what a pretty Miranda she is."

Taken off guard, Celia blushed.

"You think so?" Pride slipped into Levi's voice. "Myself, I see her more as Queen Titania of *Midsummer Night's Dream* than Miranda in *The Tempest*."

Hawthorne pushed his chair back as though he wished to make space for someone else. "You're a playwright, Mr. Thaxter?"

"I'm an actor, Mr. Hawthorne, and I've been mesmerized by this siren here—" he nodded at Celia "— and brought to these barren rocks, 'a poor player that struts and frets his hour upon the stage, and then is heard no more.' "

Celia excused herself to prepare a tea tray. Once Levi started talking about the theater, she knew she wouldn't get a word in edgewise.

While waiting for the water to boil, she wondered what it must be like to write an entire book. She'd written "Percy Allen," a short story, at school and those few pages had taken her months of painstaking work. Even then, when she'd shown it to her father, he didn't like it. Levi praised the effort, but she imagined his interest had more to do with her than with the story.

Mr. Hawthorne seemed extremely soft-spoken and retiring, but she liked his heavy-lidded eyes and broad round forehead. His moustache drooped around his full sensuous lips, giving him a mournful air that intrigued her.

The kettle whistled. She placed her best linen napkins on a flower-stenciled round tray along with the coin silver spoons her mother had given to them as a wedding gift. When she reentered the front room Nathaniel Hawthorne immediately addressed her as though he'd awaited her return. "Your husband took me to White Island to see the lighthouse this morning, Mrs. Thaxter. We met the lighthouse keeper."

Celia sat down to pour the orange pekoe. "Oh, that drunk. Was he in his right mind?" she asked, handing him a cup and saucer.

"I did notice the man was what you might call nine sails to the wind," Hawthorne admitted, continuing to stare at her for what seemed an inordinately long time. Had the baby spit up on her dress? Perhaps she was showing. She was three months pregnant again, and probably should have worn a maternity frock.

Levi placed his thumbs in his vest pockets. "The man's lost two wives already. Can't hang onto them."

Hawthorne removed a small leather notebook and a pencil stub from his waistcoat pocket, and nodded for his host to go on.

In his element, Levi obliged. "The first wife was a beauty. But her husband would go off to Portsmouth on a binge, leaving her alone for weeks at a time to care for the lighthouse best she could. We think she must have gone mad from loneliness."

Celia dreaded thinking of it. "If you want my opinion, he beat her," she said, trying to keep contempt from her voice. But it was difficult when she thought about the despicable man. More often than not he was pickled to the gills. Her father had devoted years of his life to the responsible upkeep of the light, and she hated to see it neglected.

Levi stood up and took a few paces to make sure he still held Hawthorne's attention. "Celia and I rowed over to White Island one day, hoping to strike up a friendship with her, but the poor girl had gone stark raving mad. She'd stop in mid-sentence, and sigh or sob. It was so depressing we decided not to go again. About a month later, they found her dead."

"He drove her to it," Celia interrupted, unable to curb herself. "She committed suicide."

Nathaniel Hawthorne scribbled away in his little notebook while Levi continued. "The second wife had more sense. After a few months of abject neglect, she packed her bags and left."

The young author blinked as though he'd just awakened from a long sleep. "I must be leaving too," he said, rising abruptly. Celia protested, but the quiet, unassuming writer hurried to the door, made a few quick parting remarks, and was gone.

Perplexed by Hawthorne's sudden departure, Celia sighed, and cleared away the tea things. How desperately she wanted to please Levi and make his friends welcome in their cozy island cottage.

That evening as they were getting ready for bed she still was wondering what she had done wrong when her husband kissed her tenderly on the nape of the neck and whispered in her ear, "The most famous writer in all of New England called my wife a pretty Miranda today."

Levi went over to a bookshelf and took down a leather volume embossed in gold and handed it to her. "Here, my sweet, you'd better read this before Mr. Hawthorne returns. I forgot to tell you I invited him to dinner on Sunday. He said he'd be delighted."

No sooner had Levi gone to bed than he was snoring. The baby cried. Celia took the kerosene lamp over to look at Karl. When he didn't sleep, she didn't sleep. She picked him up and sat in the rocker with the baby in one arm and Mr. Hawhorne's novel *The Scarlet Letter* propped on the other.

In the morning Celia pulled on her morning coat, suddenly overcome by a wave of nausea. If Karl was any indication of the joys of motherhood, she wasn't prepared for this second child. Their families were still supporting them, and she no longer felt in a mood to console Levi. "Maybe you could be the preacher on Star Island," she said over breakfast. "Oscar tells me they're looking for someone."

Levi merely sipped his coffee. She felt like crying most of the day, but her humor returned late that afternoon when she found the flyer for the position at Star Island on their bureau.

"I'm not an ordained minister," Levi snapped when she mentioned it again at supper.

"But you're an actor, Levi, and this might be just the role for you," she encouraged. "Besides, here's your chance to treat the fishermen to some poetry readings."

Levi wavered, and then smiled at his wife's innocent optimism. "Well, let's take a look." He read the list of qualifications aloud: "'Sweep stone chapel. Chop firewood. Mow grass. Maintain parsonage, et cetera. Deliver Sunday sermon. Teach children at Gosport. Bury the dead. Nail coffins, dig graves, shoe horses, pull teeth as need arises, et cetera.'"

Celia burst into laughter and Levi chuckled. "Oh, all right," he said. "I'll apply."

Their short stay on Star Island was one of the happiest times of their marriage. The fishing families were grateful to Levi for teaching their children and looked upon Celia and Karl as native islanders. She was sad when they had to leave, but their second child was due, and a new minister had replaced her husband. Fortunately, a friend of Lucy's, Lizzie Curzon, offered to let them live in a mill house on her family's property.

To Celia's relief, by the time their third child was on the way, Levi, with some help from his father, managed to buy them their very own home in Newtonville.

Mothering was especially difficult with Karl, who acted petulant and cranky most of the time. Celia's patience flagged as she attempted to encourage the slow-learning child. Levi had agreed to tutor Karl at home on two conditions — that he be punctual, and that he do his homework. Apprehensively, she promised for her unruly seven-year-old. She doubted that Karl would ever be able to keep up with Levi's strict routine.

One morning when Levi was out she looked up from her ironing and saw John race toward the cellar stairs. "John!" she called after him. "Why did you leave Karl alone? And what are you up to?"

"Nothing, Mama," he mumbled. Celia stoked the fire in the Portland stove, stirred the beans, and sat down. Her head ached. She wanted to rest, but the maid Doreen had gone to Boston for the day. Thankfully, baby Roland still was asleep.

John tiptoed back up the stairs. In another year or so she'd be ironing his collars and cuffs too. The noon whistle blew at the mill across the river.

All at once distressed screams came from the children's room on the second floor. "John, what are you doing to your brother?" she shouted. Sounds of the scuffle echoed down the hallway. "John," she repeated, "come out this instant!"

Caught in the act, John appeared at the head of the stairs. He crossed one foot over the other and hitched up his knickers.

"Now tell me, John Thaxter. What have you been doing to make poor Karl cry?"

John held up two flour barrel staves whittled to blunt ends. "Nothing, Mama. I didn't want him to get the rifles until they were finished. I'm John Brown on my way to raid Harper's Ferry and —."

Karl, a good foot taller than his younger brother, stood whining behind him.

"And the pewter plates you asked me to borrow?"

John took two oblong objects from his pocket. "Bullets, Mama. Bullets! One plate makes five of them. I'll be able to defend myself against the U.S. Army for at least twenty-four hours." John's face blazed triumphantly.

Celia suppressed her desire to laugh, but seeing Karl's tear-stained face, she turned suddenly angry. "You took Karl up there to play and deliberately locked him out. Now either you let him play, too, or your father — ." She paused in mid-sentence; Levi rarely reprimanded John. "Or else," she continued with a catch in her voice, "I'll give you a good whipping."

John sullenly handed Karl one of the sticks of wood and a lumpy pewter bullet.

"Like this, Karl." With his back to the stairs he brandished the play gun menacingly in his brother's face.

Karl laughed. Excited by the provocation, and imitating John, he plunged forward.

"Karl, don't!" she cried, racing toward them. Her long skirt caught at her feet as she took the stairs two at a time. But John had lost his balance and came crashing headlong toward her. Karl stood on the landing, screaming, his face flushed, swinging the toy in wide overhead circles.

She lifted John to his feet and they inched down the stairs. John groaned as she eased him onto Doreen's cot in the kitchen and tugged off his shirt. The skin was bruised where Karl had butted the blunt wood, but otherwise he seemed all right.

"How's John Brown?" Celia asked, tenderly brushing the tousellèd locks of blond hair out of his eyes.

"Karl did it," he said between clenched teeth, wrenching away from his mother. "He's crazy!"

She listened to Karl tramping up and down the hall and thought of the swallow that once had been trapped in her bedroom on White Island. Unable to find the open window, it bashed against the walls. At dawn she awoke to a crash. The bird had flown full force into the mirror. Karl needed her now, not John.

"Your brother isn't as fortunate as you are."

His voice quivered. "It doesn't make me like him any better."

The door slammed and Levi stood in the center of the kitchen, his Macintosh dripping rain. Before he had time to speak, she ran up the stairs to stop Karl's yelling.

In a stream of resentment, John told his father his version of what had happened while Celia stood with Karl trembling in the tight circle of her arms, soothing him in a gentle voice that everything was all right.

But it wasn't. Karl no longer was their son, but "that demented son of yours." Levi bellowed from below, "John could have been killed!"

She cradled Karl back and forth. "It's not true," she said defiantly. "John's not hurt. He has a few scratches, that's all."

Levi stood at the bottom of the stairs. The gaslight shone on his enraged face. "I'm taking the boy over to Doctor Moody. If anything's broken, by God, your poor Karl is going to an institution. Is that clear? An institution."

Celia made time between chores to teach her backward son his primer. One day when he was calmer than usual, she read him a poem she'd secretly been writing for several months.

"You were my inspiration, Karl," she told him.

Confused, he looked up at her.

"Remember when we dropped twigs from the bridge into the Artichoke River and wished Grammy Laighton would find them way out on Appledore Island?"

Karl's eyes filled with love at the mention of his grandmother.

"Well, this poem is about how much we miss Grammy and the Isles of Shoals."

She paused, giving in to the flood of regret welling up inside her. The previous summer Levi had been out in the skiff with her brother Oscar when a sudden squall blew up. They capsized and were swept onto some rocks near one of the islands. Celia had been looking through the binoculars and thanked God they weren't drowned. "Next time I hope you have the sense to throw a life ring in the boat," she said. But Levi insisted there would be no next time, and declared that from that day forward he would spend his summers on dry land. She thought time would change his mind. Soon, however, she realized he actually was glad for the excuse to distance himself from her.

Karl squirmed in her lap. "Read the poem again, Mama," he begged. Though Karl was a good listener, Celia craved adult company, and that afternoon she decided to take the poem with her to Curzon's Mill. Her friend Lizzie often invited artists and writers for an afternoon get-together so they could assess each other's work.

At first Celia was petrified to show the poem to Lizzie and made her promise to read it in private. But Lizzie's praise was so enthusiastic that soon Celia was writing another poem and another. It was like eating freshly baked bread. The more she ate the more she wanted.

One icy March morning she picked up *The Atlantic Monthly*

Levi had left lying on the kitchen table and thumbed through it. Longfellow, Hawthorne, Dr. Holmes, and Levi's other literary friends invariably were published in the journal, and she wondered if she'd find anyone she knew. Flipping through the advertisements, she came across a poem that looked vaguely familiar and glanced at the stanzas in astonishment —"Landlocked!" She read her poem through and when she came to the last line she was overwhelmed by pride.

But who had sent it? Months ago she'd scrawled out a copy for Levi. Had her quixotic husband understood how much this would mean to her? Or maybe Lizzie was the culprit. She'd kept the copy Celia had given her. Oscar could have given it to someone —but who? The delightful mystery had her completely baffled.

She clutched the journal to her. Baby Roland giggled and banged his spoon on the high chair while his mother swung in exuberant circles around the kitchen.

At the noon meal she propped the magazine against Levi's water glass and waited for a reaction. He glanced at her curiously, then read the poem aloud. For a moment as she listened to his rich resonant voice she was reminded of the soft summer evenings of their courtship, and the sound of the words she'd written filled her with nostalgia.

— I dream
Deliciously how twilight falls tonight
Over the glimmering water, how the light
Dies blissfully away, until I seem

To feel the wind, sea-scented, on my cheek,
To catch the sound of dusky flapping sail
And dip of oars, and voices on the gale
Afar off, calling low, my name they speak —

Levi put down the magazine and helped himself to the pot roast. Impatiently she waited for him to say something.

"It's quite good," he said. "Quite good."

"The poem or the pot roast?" she asked, overcome with excitement. "Oh Levi, you read my poem so well I couldn't help thinking you'd make a recipe for blanc mange sound like a Keats sonnet."

Levi poured some piccalilli from a cut glass castor onto his plate. "I'm flattered, but I assure you even the best actor can't make a bad poem sound good. I'm so proud that you thought to send it to *The Atlantic Monthly*."

"But Levi, you sent it, didn't you?"

"No, of course not," he said, and smiled enigmatically.

"Levi Thaxter, will you please stop joking and set my mind at rest once and for all?"

He turned to the boys. "Cross my heart," he said, dramatically making a large X on his chest. "I wish that I had sent your poem, but as far as I know, the copy you gave me still is on my desk." He whispered playfully, "Your mother has a secret admirer, boys."

Was Levi telling her the truth or putting on an act?

Suddenly, he stood and held up his glass of port. "John, Karl, I propose a toast. To your mother." He motioned for Celia to rise.

She laughed and held up her water glass.

"And to my wife," Levi said proudly, "an accomplished, and published, poet."

"To Mama! To Mama!" the boys shouted, sloshing their milk into the air.

When the hubbub had died down, Levi pulled his chair back to the table. "And now that you mention it," he added, "she's not a bad cook either."

Writing 'Til Sunrise

4

As Celia gained confidence in her writing, other facets of her life seemed to fall into place. She now took the initiative in most household decisions, and at last sought professional help for Karl.

"Mr. Thaxter has left the child's upbringing to me," she confessed to Dr. Bowditch as she sat with Karl in his front office. "I really didn't know who I could turn to. I mean, to whom I could turn." Being a writer had its drawbacks, and for Celia talking was one of them.

She clutched her handkerchief and braced herself for their conversation.

The day Karl had pushed John down the stairs, he'd disappeared. She had looked everywhere — the pantry, his room, the attic. She'd even lighted a candle and peered with terror down the two story dark shaft of the dumb-waiter. As a last resort, she was just about to turn the porcelain doorknob to her own bedroom when she heard Karl's stifled sobs.

Softly, she pushed the door ajar enough to see into the room. A pile of clothes lay carelessly at the foot of the bed, and with his back to her Karl was curled in the half-light of the drawn curtains. She started forward, then checked herself, and quietly closed the door.

Family friends frequently sent her popular journals on mental health. Many of the publications singled out masturbation as a contributing cause of insanity. Now, as she sat in the distinguished doctor's office, she had to force herself to ask his advice. Even if it wasn't what Karl had been doing, she needed a point of reference.

Dr. Bowditch swiped his brow. "Unseasonably warm for this time of year, eh, Celia?" He addressed her familiarly, she supposed, since he had been the family doctor for so long. He paced in front of the tall windows, unbuttoned his waistcoat, and spread plump hands over his vest. "Now, what did you wish to ask me? It must be terribly important to make you frown so."

"Didn't you say you had a stereoscope in your desk, Doctor?" she asked. "Karl adores looking at pictures, and it will amuse him while we talk."

"A good idea," he said, winking at Karl. "Forgive me for not thinking of it." He took out a long-handled contraption and a stack of photographic cards and handed them to Karl.

Confident that her son would be preoccupied, Celia leaned toward the doctor and lowered her voice. "I wanted to ask you — that is —." Why was this so difficult? She started again. "I've read in *The American Journal of Insanity* that masturbation is a major cause of poor mental health. I was wondering what you think?" There, she'd said it.

Dr. Bowditch smiled.

Upset by his levity, she abandoned her reticence. "I don't think this is amusing. I'm concerned for all of my sons. I've read —"

The doctor interrupted her. "Celia, do you believe everything you read?"

"But the article wasn't written by a quack. Several noted physicians have said that —"

"And you, Celia?" the doctor said. "Aren't you an authority, too? Haven't you lived with Karl's tantrums and despondency long enough to realize what applies to your own son?"

She fanned her flushed face with the handkerchief. She felt like she was suffocating. "Then what about the blood-letting and electric shock treatments? Would Karl ever be subjected to them?"

"Now I understand why you're a writer," Dr. Bowditch said. "You certainly have a keen imagination. Didn't I read a poem of yours in *The Atlantic Monthly* last issue? 'Sandpiper' — wasn't that the title? I don't pretend to understand poetry, but yours is first-rate." Then seeing that he couldn't distract her from her worries, he returned to the subject. "Now, where your Karl is concerned, I simply think fear has gotten the best of you. Blood-letting is passé. Furthermore, with Karl I think it's best that we let nature take its course." He turned toward the windows and then back to her. "Karl's in fine physical health. You'll be happy to learn that his lame leg is much better because of your swimming lessons last summer. I simply can't tolerate all this talk about institutions. And I wouldn't dream of recommending one for your son."

Tears welled in the corners of her eyes. "Mr. Thaxter said — ." Celia stopped short. If she said another word, she'd burst into tears.

The doctor had met her husband at the Saturday Literary Club and respected his talent as an actor, but he suspected Levi had little inclination for domestic affairs. Celia's growing reputation as a writer probably only compounded their marital problems.

He looked Celia straight in the eye. "Karl's a child," he told her point blank. "He'll always be a child. The sooner you accept that fact the less unhappy you'll be." When he saw her twisting a seashell bracelet nervously around her wrist, he added, "If Mr. Thaxter mentions an institution again, please have him come see me. I'll tell him exactly what I've told you. It's strange, but an outsider sometimes has more persuasive authority in these affairs."

Karl laughed loudly, bringing their talk to an abrupt close. Gleefully, he ripped one of the cards in two. Celia was about to shake the addled boy, but the doctor interceded. "No harm done. Let the child keep the card. If I'm not mistaken, I think it's a view of the Shoals."

Relieved that the interview was over, Celia kissed the doctor on both cheeks.

"Now that's more like it."

All the way back to Newtonville Karl pressed his nose to the train window while Celia rested, her eyes closed. Each clack of the wheels on the track accented a new uncertainty in her mind. She wanted to give Karl all the advantages John and Roland had, and more. But how could she be his father and mother at the same time? Levi often took the other boys with him when he traveled, and showered them with attention. But nobody cared for Karl, except her.

The following day she went to see Annie Fields in Boston. Visiting her always cheered Celia up, but to her alarm the parlor was darkened. And when Annie drew open the drapes, the once glistening white mantle and fluted columns of the colonial fireplace were coal black. "Annie, who has died?"

Her good friend sat on the divan and gestured for Celia to sit beside her. "You are so far from worldly events. Didn't Levi tell you?"

She admitted that her husband was away from home again on one of his tedious botanical expeditions.

Annie swept a hand over her black organdy dress and toward the fireplace. "This was James' idea. He was a great admirer of President Lincoln."

"Lincoln?"

She took Celia's hands. "I hope this won't be too much of a shock for you. President Lincoln was shot and killed yesterday morning. At this moment the funeral train is on its way to Springfield, Illinois, where he's to be buried."

Celia slumped dejectedly.

"Are you all right?"

She hid her face in her hands. Somehow Annie's news triggered utter despair in her. "I knew Abe Lincoln better than I know my own husband, Levi Lincoln Thaxter," she whispered in a hoarse voice. In a sudden outpouring, she told Annie about her visit with Doctor Bowditch, and her problems with Levi and Karl.

Always a sympathetic listener, Annie leaned against the satin cushions and waited. When Ceila paused, she righted herself as if she'd come to a conclusion. "You remember Mr. Whittier, don't you? I believe we introduced him to you."

Yes, Celia remembered John Greenleaf Whittier all too well. When she'd met the famous poet in the Fields' drawing room, they had talked so long and earnestly she'd missed her train that afternoon.

"Let me talk with John about Karl," she continued. "He's quite involved with the reform of prisons and mental institutions."

At the word "institution" Celia looked away.

"But that doesn't mean he believes in them," Annie immediately reassured her. "He supports the training of those less privileged than ourselves so they can become members of society. I have a hunch John Whittier's just the man who can help you."

Celia walked up the thicket-covered hill behind her cottage. The tall monument on the knoll glittered in the sun, polished and bold. It seemed foreign to that bare island where even the beaches were coarse and abrasive. She knelt in a long shadow cast by her father's grave and placed a hand on the cold smooth granite. Its coolness sounded the depths of her grief. Her mother would not let Thomas Laighton rest with the shades of death alone. And then the three of them —Oscar, Cedric, and herself — would be carried up the hill in crude island caskets. They were a family. Her other family, the one she had raised on the mainland, detested Appledore Island.

"Speak to me, Father," she whispered, her cheek pressed to the planed solid surface. As if in answer, a voice drifted from a stand of sumac.

For never comes the ship to port,
How 'er the breeze may be;
Just when she nears the waiting shore
She drifts again to sea.

She jumped up and brushed the grass from her black skirt as the sing-song lyric grew louder. John Whittier appeared on the path from Sandpiper Beach. He strode toward her, his lanky figure heightened by a natty beige top hat.

"Why, thee startled me, Mrs. Thaxter."

"Not half as much as thee startled me, John Whittier," she countered.

The famous poet had become a familiar guest at the hotel, and she felt quite at ease with his mild manner and solitary ways. Bachelor was the word most often printed in connection with his name in the society pages. He had been at the hotel long enough for Celia to notice how frequently he was alone, though he gave no indication of being lonely. That, she thought as they walked together toward her cottage, was a quality inherent in most poets. Self-consciously, she raised her hands to her hair. The summer humidity sent it into tiny irksome wisps around her forehead. They walked with the July sun beating down on them.

"The good Lord bless Japanese hop vines," he said, ducking onto the piazza surrounded by the jungle of vines that formed a pleasurable curtain of leaves against the heat. He whipped off his hat, held the screen door open for Celia, and followed her into her parlor. "I would like to talk with thee, if I may?" he asked.

"Of course, John," she said. "But wouldn't you care for some refreshment? It's terribly hot today. I fear we're in for a tantoaster."

His dark eyebrows curled like caterpillars above his deepset eyes. "What a lovely word. Of Shoals origin, no doubt?"

"I've heard it since I was a child whenever a storm was brewing." She paused and laughed. "I bet you're just dying to use it in a poem."

He rubbed his beard thoughtfully. "No, I think it belongs to thee."

She picked up a favorite Oriental fan from the table and unfolded its black lacquered stays—white silk handpainted with iris on one side. The other side depicted a long-legged water bird flying over a lake dotted with san-pans. The execution was facile but delicate, and Celia admired the talent of the unknown artist every time she unfolded it.

He took her hand and led Celia to her desk in a corner of the long room. Mechanically, she turned her wrist so that the fanned air moved in pleasant waves over her face. "I wonder why men don't use fans," she said flirtatiously and changed the fan's direction to cool the distinguished white-bearded gentleman beside her.

But John's serious demeanor didn't waver. "Mrs. Thaxter, I wish thee to understand what I am about to tell thee." Hardly a day passed when one of his articles or poems did not appear in the newspapers or magazines. She had read most of what he had written, although she had difficulty accepting his pre-war poetry drafted as a conscious political tool. Now that the war was at an end, she wondered if he realized how much his abolitionist essays had influenced its outcome. She returned his gaze with a look of respect, and was surprised to find something more than she'd anticipated.

"My heartfelt sympathies are with thee, Mrs. Thaxter, for the passing away of thy father," he said, stroking his beard. "When I lost my dear sister but two summers ago, it was hard on me. How I miss her. But I said to myself, I will love her friends better for her loss. Thou art not my sister, yet I love thee as dearly." Celia started to speak, but John continued as if he'd found his momentum. "Nor am I thy father, though surely I could pass as such."

Celia smiled. Although John was twice her age, in no way did he compare with her father. Up to now she'd never thought of him except as a much-revered mentor. The more he said, the more she wondered. And how she craved an understanding companion. This summer her husband was at Mount Desert in Maine with Roland and John. Even her father's death had brought Levi to Appledore Island for only a week. Her mother had been bed-ridden most of the summer. Celia had taken over the work-load at the hotel and it was too much for her. She felt like she was on the verge of collapse, and the renowned poet's support came just when she needed a shoulder to lean on.

John Greenleaf Whittier had never been a rich man and, in fact, Celia had heard rumors that his financial position early on had dissuaded him from marriage. Yet she was sure that had he decided to marry, he never would have deserted his wife as Levi had deserted her. And he would have been a kind and understanding father to Karl. If it hadn't been for John's concerned recommendation, Karl would have had no schooling at all. Yes, when all was said and done, John Whittier had many qualities she admired.

"And so, dearest Celia," he concluded, "I would hope thee to consider me an affectionate and devoted friend."

What she then said thoroughly surprised her as she heard it echo through her parlor. "How I appreciate your words, John. I know you were only going to stay through July, but couldn't you stay through the summer? Mr. Thaxter will be on the mainland, and my mother and I would find your company most welcome."

He was telling her that he would give her invitation serious thought when a distinct cough came from somewhere in the parlor. Dismayed, Celia glanced around the room. An entire regiment could have hidden there without being seen. Every inch of wall space was covered with photographs, paintings, maps, and engravings. The tops of the book shelves, mantle, and tables were crowded with vases of flowers and stacks of books. Ottomans and chairs were pushed into the disorder, leaving a wide corridor of hardwood floor scattered with worn rugs. The grand piano was crammed into an L-shaped alcove and served as still another repository for flowers and books.

Although Celia didn't like it, she was used to intruders from the hotel sneaking into her parlor to solicit autographs. She found the culprit reclined on a plump sofa pillow pretending to read a book.

"Oh, is that you, Mrs. Thaxter?" the woman asked with feigned innocence. "I was so engrossed I didn't realize anyone was here." Seeing Celia's growing anger, the woman swung her feet from the ottoman to the floor and offered a limp hand. "I'm Mrs. Lydia Stoddard, and I've been looking forward to meeting you."

"Then I suggest, Mrs. Stoddard, that you catch me when I'm at the hotel. This is my parlor, and only my closest friends are allowed to visit me here." When the woman looked as if she would not be rebuffed, Celia added, "and then, only if I extend an invitation."

The woman pouted, her green eyes flashing. "I thought since we were fellow writers you wouldn't mind. In fact, I was hoping you would let me interview you, and I could write a little sketch —."

"Mrs. Stoddard," Celia said, raising her voice, "I assure you that we have nothing in common, and I do mind!"

John evidently had decided that Quaker silence was his best recourse. The woman picked up a parasol from the couch, and twirling the handle back and forth like a cat pawing a beached minnow, she headed for the screen door. Before making her final exit, she turned dramatically and pronounced, "Don't worry, Mrs. Thaxter, I can keep a secret." She paused, and as they glowered at each other, added, "Well, for a little while."

5

Toward the end of August the crowds thinned at the hotel, leaving Celia more time at her cottage where every guest room still was occupied. She didn't think of the occupants as guests but fellow writers and artists like herself intent on their creative pursuits.

In the evening as they gathered for informal readings and concerts, she grew accustomed to John's bemused attention, but always mindful of propriety, they continued to address each other by surname when in company.

One sultry evening, William Mason sat in the lamplight and played a Chopin nocturne while beside him artist Ellen Robbins turned pages. The smell of honeysuckle drifted through the open windows, and frosted globe gas lamps lighted the faces a soft rose hue.

Celia adjusted the flame in a lamp over her desk. The poem she was writing seemed almost composed by the music she was hearing. She looked up a moment. People like Ellen and William filled her with such joy and satisfaction. All at once John slipped through the French doors at the other end of the room and stood silent yet conspicuous—to her at least.

She put a hand to her forehead, shading her eyes with curved fingers so he wouldn't see her. She tried to concentrate on the stanza:

The quiet room, the flowers, the perfumed calm,
The slender crystal vase, where all aflame
The scarlet poppies stand erect and tall,
Color that burns as if no frost could tame,
The shaded lamplight glowing over all,
The summer night a dream of warmth and balm.

She dipped her pen into the cut-glass ink well, but William had concluded his impromptu concert with a lively polonnaise, and the spell was broken.

Ellen proposed that it was much too lovely out to stay indoors, and someone suggested a stroll in the moonlight.

They left by twos and threes. A few bade Celia good-night. But most of them were aware that when she was at her desk, which jesting friends referred to as her "throne," she wasn't to be disturbed.

She sighed and once more bent over the poem.

"Might I convince thee that one's work is never fresher than when reviewed at dawn?"

"John?" Celia half-questioned, half-beckoned to him. "Aren't you afraid you'll meet up with Phillip Babb's ghost in the moonlight?"

"Oh, that rogue," he scoffed, holding out her paisley shawl, for even on summer nights the breeze rarely let up near the shore. "I'm not afraid of him. Now wasn't he that buccaneer who lived on the Shoals?"

"Buccaneer, tavernkeep, and island butcher. He also ran a family bowling alley," she added.

They turned opposite the direction taken by the others. John drew his arm through the crook of Celia's elbow, and they made their way down the hill toward the pier, stopping at her garden. "I'll pick you a boutonnière," she said, casting about the silvery blossoms for a flower to put in his empty buttonhole. She broke the stem of a bachelor button and fastened the blue cornflower in his lapel.

"Too appropriate," he commented, smiling at her.

They continued on the path over the cliffs and down to Babb's Cove. The moonlight danced like garnets on the water and silhouetted the White Island lighthouse. The catwalk from the lighthouse to the cottage glistened in the moonlight, and she thought of the days she 'd played in the belly of that leviathan.

How calm it was tonight compared with the ferocious storms she'd experienced as a child. She still remembered her terror at seeing the china on the floor, doors unhinged, and sides of mutton tossed around the cellar. And yet the next day the sun rose with such warmth and intensity. How unpredictable nature could be.

Lost in their own thoughts, they'd come to Babb's Cove, and John gallantly laid down his waistcoat for them to sit on. "Tell me this story of Babb," he prodded, leaning back in his shirtsleeves. "I'm interested in this ghost."

She clasped her arms around her knees and stared past Babb's rock. "Forgive me, Mr. Whittier," she said, hoping her formality might conceal the tenderness that had been playing her at odds all evening, "my mind seems to have been elsewhere."

"And where was that?"

"On the delightful isolation of childhood," she admitted. "Can you imagine, this summer we actually bedded and boarded three-hundred guests at Appledore Hotel!"

"And thy nature longs for solitude?"

Celia rested her chin on her knees. "Sometimes," she answered. "Sometimes I'm so—." She yearned for understanding, but she stopped herself in mid-sentence, unwilling to let her emotions get the best of her.

"—So?"

"Oh, nothing. Now, about Babb. He's appeared to several people at the hotel. They describe him as a husky man wearing a blood-stained butcher's apron, a wide leather belt, and a sharply honed cutlass which he wields to intimidate Hog Islanders."

"Celia," he reprimanded. "Methinks thou hast changed the subject."

"Not now, John. It's too beautiful a night to spoil with regrets."

He placed his hand momentarily on her bent head as though bestowing a benediction. She paused, and then continued telling her story. "Appledore was Hog Island before my father bought it. Imagine a resort called Hog Hotel!" She laughed nervously and rushed on, hoping to make a clean slate of their conversation. "Where we're sitting is where Babb dug for treasure which Captain Kidd was to have buried. Babb and his mate, Ambrose Gibbon, did find the chest. But when they forced it open, sulfurous smoke and red-hot horseshoes flew into their faces."

John laughed, and Celia joined him. Having told the tale more than once, she lowered her voice as prescribed for ghost stories. "You may laugh, John Greenleaf Whittier, but many a night I've waited up with fearful guests who swear they met Babb's ghost on the very path we took to this cove."

John chuckled. "Dear Celia, thou hast a most charming way about thee."

"I know you don't believe in spirits, John," she said, shrugging off the compliment and preserving her tone of banter, "but it's no reason to disbelieve those that do. One poor woman checked out of the hotel the very day after she'd checked in. She was so upset by the apparition she had seen that she wouldn't so much as wave a handkerchief as the *Pinafore* left the dock. She told me that the despicable ghost actually chased her back to the hotel, blaspheming and brandishing his cutlass the entire way. The woman was pale as a ghost herself when we revived her with smelling salts." Celia smiled, completely relaxed. Telling island stories always amused her.

John clasped her hand. "Do write these tales down. Thou art a born storyteller."

The warmth of his hand and still another compliment brought a flush to her cheeks. "Oh, but I can't," she told him, standing up and pulling them both to their feet. "I've only written poetry."

He held her firmly by both shoulders and persisted. "I know thee, Celia Thaxter. Set thy mind and pen to the task."

His head bent down as she tilted her neck back to look up at him. His hand slipped down her arm to her waist, encircling her. The other hand lifted her chin. Before she could object, their lips met, sealing an affection that had been deepening through the summer. For one delusive moment she relinquished her body to his embrace while the pinks she wore against her bodice were crushed into fragrance.

Then with all the strength she could muster, she pushed John's broad shoulders at arm's length, regaining her composure. She knew exactly where romance could lead, and she wanted none of it.

"Mr. Whittier, may I remind you that I am a married woman."

John stepped back. "Mrs. Thaxter," he said, "I humbly beg thy pardon. Thy intelligence and charm carried me completely away." He picked up his coat and hurried after her. Their stilted words hung in the air between them like a script written by someone else. If only they had met sooner, she thought, they could have been lovers like Elizabeth and Robert Browning. If only they had been introduced sooner—.

He looked askance at her as they walked briskly by the swimming hole and toward her cottage. The grasshoppers arched through the air as her skirt swished over the tall grass.

Suddenly, Celia broke the silence, her resolution to keep aloof thrown to the winds, when a bat swooped out of the darkness. "John, duck!" she shouted, grabbing his arm and pulling him toward her.

The bat fluttered past his forehead. "God's Great Mercy," John swore, staring after the ugly creature.

The tension dissipated and they walked on, stopping short of the piazza of her cottage. "I petted a bat once when I was a child. It seemed so soft and furry, but it bit me. So much for appearances," she said, glancing at him to see if he caught her meaning.

John drew near but didn't touch her. "I admire and respect thee, Celia Thaxter. Please think of me as thy trustworthy friend."

Both sorry and glad they still were reading the stiff, reproachable script, she said good-night and they parted, each absorbed in the frustration of such a compromise.

6

A thick fog shrouded the islands. Celia opened the garden gate and wound past the man-size hollyhocks and wisteria vines twisted around the fence. Although her garden badly needed rain, she hoped that the fog would lift and not spoil the day's festivity. Prior to closing, the kitchen staff were busy cleaning the pantry and dining room. and so a picnic was spread on long tables on the lawn. Invariably, her mother decided that leftovers weren't sufficient and whipped up half a dozen pound cakes to go with hand-cranked vanilla ice cream. Volunteers were sent around the island in search of the last blueberries of the season as a final topping to the dessert. The picnic would be followed by a farewell cotillion played by the Appledore Band from sundown to midnight.

A catbird hopped to a fence post near Celia's head and chortled a long ridiculous good morning, wagging his tail during the more grandiose cadenzas. She whistled back such a close imitation that the bird cocked its head in astonishment and flew away.

She worked patiently, staking up a clump of energetic dahlias stealing over the lobelia border. She watered a thirsty scarlet rose, talking to it as she did so. "You look so thirsty. Well, we don't want it to rain today so please be patient." Patches of blue sky appeared and the sun shone through. She must get back to the parlor to draw the curtains and capture some of the cool morning air for her guests.

Not many flowers to cut so late in the season. Purple asters, of course, and a few Japanese zinnias. They were a new variety she'd ordered from Faxon's Seed Company in Boston, and she was pleased with them. Her arms laden with flowers, she returned to the cottage, while imagining the world as her private sanctuary, and she, the high priestess chosen to worship while the others slept.

Each dawn she performed the same comforting ritual. First, she watered the twinberry vines growing in dishes of moss on the parlor tables. Next, she discarded the wilted flowers in the fluted vases on the mantle, replacing them with freshly cut bouquets. To her, a room without flowers was like a room without chairs. She remembered someone joking once that Celia Thaxter would rather die than step on a flower. Karl already had gone to decorate the ballroom and help carry the tables.

After working at her desk for a few hours, she walked over to the hotel. She was determined to shrink her waistline before returning to Newtonville for winter, and the best method she could think of was to eat no breakfast. On the way she eyed a few slim bathing beauties at the pool. It made her cringe to imagine how ludicrous she would look in their bathing costumes. They wore suits of turkey red hiked up with sashes, full drawers, long black stockings, and straw hats. An admiring gentleman snapped their picture behind his folding camera.

Celia hurried across the tennis lawn to the hotel and nodded perfunctorily at the few guests conversing on the piazza extending the length of the hotel. The mail was delivered from the steamer to the hotel three times a day and a good share of it was for her. At the desk in the lobby Cedric greeted her and slid a packet of letters over the black walnut counter.

"Not too much today, Sister," he said. "Things are slowing down." They exchanged happy glances at the prospect, and she took the letters to the large plate glass windows fronting the steamer launch. Except for a few cigar-smoking gentlemen with their noses in *The Boston Transcript*, the main lobby was empty.

She pulled a rocker toward the window and sorted through the mail. A letter from one of the children's magazines she wrote for, and a joint letter from her sons. Nothing from Levi. A note from Dr. Bowditch regretting that he hadn't been able to get away from Boston that August. A letter from Annie. It was thick and tempting.

Several women were staying at Celia's cottage this summer, but she wasn't very close to any of them. Ellen Robbins seemed bright and friendly. Celia liked her, but so did Mr. Mason, and she spent most of her time with him.

She tore open Annie's envelope and squinted at the fine handwriting:

Dearest Sandpiper,

We just have learned that Charles Dickens will be reading in Boston this winter. The dates aren't set exactly as he also will give readings in New York and Philadelphia. James and I are most excited. It promises to be the Literary Event of the decade — if not the century.

I do hope that you will be in Newtonville this winter. I am counting on you to represent the Shoals at a dinner party I plan to give in Mr. Dickens' honor. I know you have followed his literary career avidly. Remember how we waited for the ship from England to come into Boston Harbor with each new installment of Little Nell, and how interminable the wait seemed?

I have personal matters I must confide. Imagine my amazement when one of those busy-bodies that frequently show up at social gatherings handed me the society page from her county newspaper — with which I'm not familiar — and proceeded to tell me, before I had a chance to read it, that John Whittier is on the brink of holy matrimony!

Celia re-read the last line and put the letter down, staring past the bathing pool and beyond to a luffing white sail. Many times John had told her that he was a confirmed bachelor. What did this news mean?

Both you and I know this is false rumor. However, I must own that it concerns you.

She stood up and refolded the letter. Two fashionable women had turned from the hotel clerk, and, recognizing their hostess, rushed toward her. She tried to reach the door before they intercepted her, but it was no use. One of them decked from head to toe in lavender ruffles called out, "A lovely day for the grand finale, isn't it, Mrs. Thaxter?" She tittered while her friend, staring from beneath the feathers of a snowy owl, nodded agreement at her every word.

The woman with the hour-glass figure leaned in Celia's direction. "I was just telling my companion, Mrs. Adelaide Brewster, that our dear Rose of the Isles looks in the very bloom of health." Celia wished them a good day, but the women already had thrust their autograph albums toward her. "My friend and I," the woman chattered on, "were so hoping that you would write a verse from one of your poems in our albums."

Karl came running up the steps, entreating his mother to let him go with her brother to Smutty-Nose to pick up the crabmeat. His childish interruption, infused with the enthusiasm of a nine-year-old, completely perplexed the two women, and they stepped away as if to dissociate themselves from an embarrassing situation. Celia excused herself, hugging Karl conspicuously until they reached her cottage. Only after she'd escaped the women did she give him permission to go with Cedric to see the Norwegian fishermen.

Relieved to be in her parlor once more, she finished reading Annie's long letter.

> *I don't know who wrote the newspaper account, but she had recently visited the Shoals, and insinuated that you and John often were seen together. The gossip column implied that it was only a matter of time before you would be divorced and married to John Whittier! The scandal sheet was signed with the initials L.S.*

Celia choked with rage. She had known that despicable woman was up to no good the moment she laid eyes on her. If ever she met Lydia Stoddard again, she would throttle her.

Of course, I spoke my mind to the silly woman who gave me the clipping and I told her she should be reading The Atlantic Monthly and not such idle chitchat. Of course, she wasn't too pleased with my advice, and I'm afraid I made quite a few enemies before the punch was served.

Celia, my dearest friend in all the world, you must not let this upset your equilibrium. Some women have absolutely nothing to do with their lives but to disturb the lives of others. I only wish I were there to remind you how fickle the public is and to entreat you to disregard printed slander of this nature.

Everyone knows, of course, that you are a married woman with three children and that John Whittier is at his autumnal equinox. I can only assure you, Celia, that whoever L.S. is, she has left herself open to ridicule far greater than she intended for you and John. My true friend, I trust that you are well. My warmest regards to your mother.

As ever, your owlette,
Annie

P.S. James and I miss you terribly.

Celia walked onto the cottage piazza. The horizon was radiantly clear; she could see Po Hill near Amesbury where John lived. But John wasn't on Po Hill. He was right there on Appledore, and every morning he received at least twenty-five letters from friends and devoted admirers. Sooner or later he would learn of the awful hearsay. How could she possibly face him at the picnic that afternoon? And Levi — what if the horrid tales were to reach him? Should she confess to her husband that on a moonlit night

Mr. Whittier had kissed her, and she had kissed him back? Would he believe they were only friends if he saw them together?

Tired to tears, she climbed the stairs to her bedroom. The pretty summer dress that her mother had made for her thirty-second birthday was laid out on the bed. She'd been so busy that summer, she'd worn the gown only once. It was of musk-colored chiffon with plain lace sleeves, trimmed in light blue with a blue velvet belt. Beside it Celia had placed her seashell necklace and a silver crescent on a small tortoise shell comb, a gift from Annie. When she wore it, she thought of the spiritual bond she shared with her friend.

She picked up the comb, stroking its slender curve in her long fingers. When she had placed it there early that morning, she had been as carefree and expectant as a child. How quickly joy turned to grief. Her shoulders shook, and she collapsed onto the bed, burying her wet face in the crumpled dress.

7

Celia awoke to a knock on the door and her mother's concerned voice. She rubbed her sleep-filled eyes, unsure what day it was and why her mother looked so anxious.

"Are you all right?" Eliza asked, sitting beside her on the bed. "The tub races are over and they're already eating supper on the lawn. What would you like me to fetch you? Do you need some Lydia Pinkham's?"

Celia smiled. No matter how old she was, her mother would always treat her as an only daughter. "No," she said. "I'm just tired."

Eliza sighed and felt her daughter's forehead with a cool hand. "I know how you look forward to this day, and it's turned out so well. Everyone is asking for you." She poured a tumbler of water and handed it to her. "You really must eat something, dear. I suppose you poets think you don't need to eat," Eliza Laighton said crossly. "Now I'm sending a tray up and I want you to eat something."

Celia rubbed her mother's arm affectionately. "All right," she acquiesced, settling back on the pillows.

Eliza was gone only five minutes when another knock sounded on the door. "Just a moment," she called, unprepared for the arrival of the promised tray quite so soon. She got up, ran a brush through her long loose hair, hung the rumpled party dress in the wardrobe, and returned to sit on the bed. Ill or not, she didn't want the servants to see her in complete disarray.

"Come in," she called, preparing herself for a second lecture from her mother's adoring kitchen staff.

The door opened slowly to the clinking of dishes. Since her room was dark with the drapes half-drawn, she illuminated the kerosene lamp, glad for the few seconds it took to remove the chimney and light the wick. To her amazement John Whittier stood at the door sill.

"Thy mother persuaded me to bring thee a part of the banquet," he said, remaining at the threshold as if not quite sure he should enter. "We were missing thy company, and I volunteered to come and heal thy ailing spirits."

Celia beckoned to him but remained silent, saddened by the thought that their friendship was being marred by the whims of an eavesdropping journalist.

John stared at her over the wicker tray filled with pitchers, plates, cruets, and castors. "Why, what is the matter, Celia? The color has gone completely from thy cheeks. "

She cleared the books from her bedside table. "Please, John," she said, "put that down before you drop it."

"I don't claim to be Doctor Oliver Wendell Holmes, but it does not take a man of medicine to observe that thou art not thyself." He pulled up a chair. "May I join thee? Eating alone does little good for the spirit, especially when boisterous merry-making is taking place right outside thy window."

She managed a wan smile, but his kindness only increased her remorse, and she felt even more guilty for liking the poet.

John removed the cover from a plate heaped with crabmeat salad, devilled eggs, baked ham and cornmeal toads. "I have the strictest orders," he said, handing her a fork and a plate, "that thou art to eat it all, or no dessert."

Eyes downcast, she played with her food, afraid that if she were to look into his craggy, beloved face, the tears would spill over.

He took a bite, then stopped eating. "My dear Celia, what can be troubling thee? I have never seen thee so dispirited. Is it because of the other night? If so, I apologize from the bottom of my heart."

She shook her head. She had been brought up to understand that holding back a truthful answer was as serious an offense as telling a lie. Her hand reached under her pillow for the folded sheets of stationery. "I received a letter from Annie Fields today," she told him.

"Pray, and what did she have to say that has upset thee so?"

Celia shuffled through the pages until she came to the part about them and handed it to John. He moved the letter into the lamplight, and it seemed an eternity while he read it. He folded the page and, smiling resolutely, handed it back to her.

"And this is the nonsense that has taken thy appetite?" he asked.

She looked down at the coverlet. He hadn't reacted at all to the letter. She dabbed at the crab salad with her fork.

"My dear Celia," he said gently. "This is mere gossip. Save thy energy for thy writing."

She took a bite of salad, then another.

He dipped a small silver spoon into the mustard jar and slathered a piece of ham. "I guess the reporters have hounded me for so long that I've become immune to their silly stories. This is by no means the first speculation concerning my celibate status."

John said this with such manly pride that Celia could not help smiling. Suddenly, she was famished.

Satisfied as a shepherd that has saved one of his sheep, John flipped the porcelain stopper off a blob-top bottle of ginger beer. A spurt of amber liquid shot into the air as he shoved his chair backward. She grabbed her tumbler and thrust it beneath the frothing beer erupting like Old Faithful all over the carpet and John's cheviot suit.

She burst into uncontained laughter. John looked grimly at the half of a bottle that remained and poured it into her tumbler. "It seems that I have cheered thee at the expense of making a frightful mess." He wiped the sticky foam from his waistcoat with a hotel napkin and stooped to mop the rest off the carpet.

Celia jumped to her feet, pulling him with her. "John, I'll take care of that." She took the napkin from him. "Besides, my poor Karly has been working on the decorations for the dance all day, and I know that he'll be disappointed if you don't show up."

They stood in the cozy circle of light, he in his best clothes, and she in her dressing gown and stocking feet. She felt that they were seconds close yet years apart.

"I promise to leave thee on one condition." He paused, looking down at her. "Thy absence simply would lend credence to rumors. Besides, I don't want to spend the entire evening with the men on the piazza."

How could she possibly refuse when he looked at her like that? "All right, John. I'll be there."

He picked up the tray to leave, but had second thoughts and returned to the circle of light, hesitating as if to reconsider, and then blurted out, "Were I to change my bachelorhood, beloved Celia, thy ears would be the first to hear of it."

Usually she disliked getting dressed up, but this evening she paid special attention, dusting a pink powder puff over her shiny nose, and rubbing a slight tinge of rouge into her cheeks. The dress really should be pressed, but it was too late to wait for the sad iron to heat up. Besides, the dress fit so perfectly that the wrinkles would soon hang out. She plaited her long brassy hair and looped it in a crown around her head.

Strains of the *Opera House Waltz* floated over the newly mowed lawn, and she stopped in the moonlight to look up at the five-story yellow hotel. The dark lifeless upper story windows seemed hauntingly empty next to the gaily lighted ballroom. On the piazza, silhouettes of gentlemen smoking were outlined in the backlighted double doors. Two bustled ladies stood away from the smoke, their combined figures casting shadow pictures in the shaft of light.

Celia gathered up her skirt and climbed the piazza stairs. Karl met her halfway, his face flushed with excitement. "Mama, Mama, come, I want you to see. " He skipped ahead, nearly crashing into a gentleman coming down the stairs as they went up. Celia stopped to apologize. Guests nodded and greeted her as she swept past.

The band had stopped playing and the dancers crowded onto the piazza for some air. At the doors Celia caught up with her son, and was just reminding him that he should go to bed by ten o'clock when a contrary voice disagreed.

"Now, Mother, that's much too early for a boy Karl's age," John said, poised against the railing.

Karl grinned and grabbed John Whittier's hand gratefully. Celia shook her head at their complicity. "Oh well, I do suppose he could stay up until midnight."

John gestured a place beside him on the railing, but impatient, Karl was tugging her toward the door, and with a helpless backward glance, she tripped along behind her excited son.

The varnished oak dance floor gleamed in the light of the chandeliers, their bell-shaped globes shimmering on the swags of sea-green crepe streamers looped overhead. The band members, dressed in dark twill with gold buttons and braid, were milling around the punch table decorated with silver fern dishes filled with flowers and placed on beveled mirrors. Crystal fruit and silver nut dishes surrounded two huge cut-glass punch bowls, and to the side, reception chairs were staggered with wicker chairs under the fluted bracket lamps from which hung large conch shells filled with sweet william.

Celia hugged her son enthusiastically. "Why Karly, you and Cedric have created a masterpiece!" He beamed at her praise.

"The shells were my idea. Do you like them? Do you?" Karl tugged at her hand.

"Yes, Karl, I do." She nodded to members of the band who were sipping punch, their faces flushed from the nonstop playing of trombones and euphoniums. "Indeed, Karly," she repeated, distracted by a gentleman in a floral waistcoat and muttonchops. He stood by one of the open windows and spat tobacco juice onto the porch outside.

"Oh, dear," she muttered. "Are the cuspidors on the piazza, Karly? The maids will have a devil of a time getting the stains off the wood if they aren't in place."

"I saw Oscar do it, Mama."

The boy so wanted to please her. He was all spruced up in long pants and a band bow tie. He wasn't a bad looking boy. Who would suspect that he must be told what to do every minute of the waking day?

Karl led her to the raised stage at the opposite end of the ballroom. Only last week a guest actually had suggested they turn the mammoth room into a roller skating rink. Celia shuddered. What you had to put up with when you ran a hotel.

From the first day the hotel had opened, her father had tried to keep up with the times, and every entertainment found at other resorts was available at Appledore—billiards, bowling, band music, ballroom dancing, a bar in the basement. But roller skating was the limit, and she and her brothers felt sure that if their father were alive, he would agree.

She stood before the stage decorated with a tissue paper banner lettered in gold: *APPLEDORE, 1866.* The music stands were garlanded in hop vines and pink satin ribbons. A line of single ladies clutching apple-green, velvet-covered dance programs decorated with small seashells, queued against the bank of windows. Many of the women were attracted to the Appledore Hotel because it was self-contained and incidental expenses such as livery fees were minimal. In addition, Celia had to admit that they came to see her, if only at a distance. Tonight, several of them wore shell necklaces in imitation of the one she had worn at the last cotillion. No doubt at that very moment one of them was whispering sympathetic platitudes about her son Karl, or remarking that they'd seen her in John Whittier's company a great deal that summer.

Celia squeezed her lace handkerchief into a ball, and stepped aside to let the band members pass, addressing each one by name. She drew the band leader aside and requested two songs—

Beware! Take Care! to a verse by Longfellow, and Whittier's popular refrain, the *Contraband of Port Royal.*

After the musicians had settled, the conductor rapped his baton on the edge of a stand and roused the fife, clarinet, piano, and trombone in a lively polka. In seconds, the floor once more was a mass of color that whirled around her like a carousel. After that, gentlemen formed at one end of the ballroom, and ladies at the other. Celia made her way to the open window sill and let the refreshing breeze blow on her face.

"Come stroll with me on the piazza," John said, peering in as Celia peered out.

With relief, she left the ballroom and stepped into the cool night air. He offered her his arm, and slowly they meandered down the long veranda, glancing fondly at each other from time to time. When they reached the main hotel, they continued strolling in the shadows. On the lawn in front of the steps, a group of excited youngsters had set up wickets with candles on them to play croquet. The candles flickered and twinkled as the rumble behind them grew louder.

"Those dancers certainly are raising the roof," John said.

"It's thunder, John." She pointed out a flash of lightning over the mainland. "We're in for a nor'easter."

He smiled. "Thy observances put me to shame."

She squeezed his arm affectionately. "The weather is a matter of no small consequence on the Shoals." Their footsteps resonated on the boardwalk, and a louder peal of thunder reverberated as the wind picked up and gusted over the balustrade. They turned back to the lighted dance hall. She moved from one group to another. As hostess she was expected to introduce and be introduced, and ask the guests if they had enjoyed their visit. They gathered around her like fish to bait. Only during a brief lull did she spot John weaving toward the bandstand. The fashionable ladies she had escaped that morning led her to a table to sign their albums. This done, again she looked for John and was surprised to see him bounding up the steps of the stage. He leaned over the piano player. What on earth was he doing? In a wide arc Celia again made her rounds as hostess, ending up at the opposite side of the room. The music stopped abruptly and one of the band members stood near the piano. Aware that this was to be a vocal number, the dancers moved off the floor. John jostled back into the crowd as the tenor sang.

I long for Jeanie with the day-dawn smile
Radiant in gladness, warm with winning guile.
I hear her melodies like joys gone by,
Sighing round my heart o'er the fond hopes that die.

Celia dared not look at John, although he now stood but a few yards away.

Sighing like the night wind and sobbing like the rain,
Wailing for the lost one that comes not again
Ah! I long for Jeanie and my heart bows low
Never more to find her where the bright waters flow.

The guests applauded, and slowly drifted back onto the dance floor. Celia stood in confused wonder as John walked toward her, his dark eyes attracted to her as if by a magnet. Before she knew what was happening, he had drawn her to him and they were in each other's arms.

8

Celia's intention to sit down and work on the Shoals book she'd promised to write vanished in a wave of unpacking, dusting, and cooking. Worried by the regularity of bills and irregularity of funds to pay them, she sent poetry submissions to *Scribner's, Harper's, The Independent,* and *The Century*. Acceptances outnumbered rejections, and she felt blessed to do what she most enjoyed in order to keep house and home together.

Levi was ill. The doctor had told him that severe New England winters were playing havoc with his lungs; he should seriously consider moving to a milder climate. But that was out of the question now that he was completely bedridden.

Celia had left her desk to bake him some scones and make a pot of tea. Levi glared at her as she brought in the tray, his face ashen. "Set it down, woman, and leave me in peace," he growled. "Not that you care that I have to cancel my presentation of Robert Browning."

She smoothed the bedcovers and, trying to appease him, said, "There will be other readings. Your health comes first." She pulled up a chair, thought of John on that bright summer day when he had pulled up a chair at her bedside. In one brief month she had resumed her depressing role as the dutiful wife. "Do drink your tea while it's hot."

"No reading, no money," Levi said to the wall.

"We'll get by. *The Atlantic Monthly* is printing two poems next month, and Mr. Whittier has given me the name of an editor who wishes to print a few. We won't starve."

Just mentioning Whittier's name cheered her up. But if anything, Levi looked worse. Whenever she talked about her poetry, he shut up like a barnacle at low tide.

She opened the window and the chill November wind drew the curtains into the room. Levi pulled the afghan under his chin and coughed spasmodically. "You and your infernal fresh air, Celia," he snarled between fits of coughing. "Do you want to send me to an early grave?"

Gently, she propped him up and held a tin pan under his mouth to spit in, but with a wild gesture he knocked it away. "Woman, you tire my patience. I know what you're thinking. You're thinking I'm no good." He took a gulp of the tea, then pushed aside the tray, leaving the scones cold and untouched. "You're thinking, 'Poor Levi, he'll always be a failure.' "

She moved away from the bed and across the room to stoke the fire. She had grown used to his jealousy of her writing, and even to his repudiation of the Isles of Shoals, but never would she accustom herself to this abject self-pity.

When his eyes were closed, she tiptoed toward the bed to get the tray. Suddenly, he grabbed her arm as she reached over the coverlet. He had never physically struck her, but his words dealt a heavy blow. "Fat old biddy," he snapped. "Even on tiptoe you sound like an elephant."

Celia let the brass knocker fall twice on the door at 37 Charles Street. The Fields' maid answered, recognized her, and opened it wide, smiling welcome. How alive and bright she appeared compared to the dimwitted help Celia always seemed to find.

The maid took her brown worsted cape and gloves, and stood behind her while she unpinned her plain brown bonnet. Celia was much more comfortable without fashion's horrid bird nests perched on top of her head. She wended her way behind the maid and down the hall to the double library doors at the same moment Annie was coming out, and they fell into each other's affectionate embrace.

Annie took Celia's arm and ushered her toward an unprepossessing woman about ten years older than themselves. "I'm Lucy Larcom," she said, extending her hand. "I believe we met once on the Isles of Shoals."

The women exchanged pleasantries as they entered the massive library with west windows overlooking a bend in the Charles River. They sat around a large mahogany tea table scattered with half-open books and various mementos from abroad — everything, in fact, except tea.

"You must call me Lucy," the woman said, her taffeta dress rustling while she moved her hands in flamboyant gestures. "I dislike being Miss Larcom. It reminds me I'm a teacher. I'm living in Lowell now. I just can't seem to get away from the mills. I was a spinner when I was a girl, you know. But tell me all about yourself. I've read your poems and think the sea images are every bit as lovely as a Turner seascape. I adore

Turner, don't you?" Before Celia could answer, the woman was off on another tangent.

"I'm here to help Annie organize the Dickens' banquet, but I have to admit that I have secondary motives for my visit, or didn't Annie tell you?" Celia waited politely. "What I mean is that I certainly would like you to submit some of those splendid poems of yours to *Our Young Folks*. We don't pay much, and I'm new to the magazine, but Mr. Whittier and I already are discussing a collaboration on some children's poetry anthologies. You've met Mr. Whittier, of course? Isn't he the kindest, most admirable man in the world? We've known each other for years."

Celia took a deep breath since the woman facing her wasn't going to.

"I met John several years before the war," she rushed on. "He was writing his abolitionist essays. Let me see, I think it was around '44 just before I left for Illinois to teach on that God-forsaken frontier. I'd read his essays on social reform, and having worked in the mills as I did, we had a lot of ideas in common. But where was I? Oh, yes. The magazine. Well, to plan each issue I have to ride over to see John in Amesbury. But, of course, I'm not alone. The adoring pilgrims always are dropping by for an autograph right in the middle of our editorial discussions. He usually takes them out to see his rose garden. Have you seen it? I know how you love flowers."

Lucy Larcom looked like a school marm, but there was something more about her that held Celia's attention. "No, I've never been to Amesbury," she said, thinking it was rather brash for the woman to admit that she'd gone to see John unchaperoned. But then, mill girls had that kind of reputation. Released from the strictures of home by their four dollar weekly wages, they seemed to think they could do anything they pleased.

"It's difficult for me to get away from the house," she said pointedly. "I have three growing boys."

Annie arranged the pillows behind them as if to bolster themselves for another siege of conversation.

"My friendship with John has caused me a deal of heartache," Lucy continued. "You and Annie have been happily married, but let's face it—I'm an old maid. I've always had to fend for myself."

Celia shifted uncomfortably against the pillows. How quickly people took the lives of others at face value. And besides, what was the woman leading up to?

"Now ladies, you must promise that what I say won't pass beyond these walls." Not waiting for a response, Lucy Larcom continued disclosing her most intimate secrets. "As I said, being single and on my own, I decided to tempt fate. I popped the question, since John hadn't asked me. To make a long story short, he refused. But in the meantime, someone from the newspaper wrote that we were engaged. John was furious. He wrote them back that he had no intentions of the kind. This all happened some twenty years ago. I suppose I should have known better. At that time he was courting several women, and I learned later that he'd proposed to at least four of them. They all turned him down. Leave it to Lucy Larcom to want what nobody else would take."

The woman was too much for Celia. "John Whittier hardly can be thought of as the Don Juan you're portraying, Miss Larcom," she said coldly. "And as for his proposals to four women, don't you think you're exaggerating?"

Lucy appraised Celia for a moment, then in a calculating, teacherly tone she proclaimed, "Obviously, many people don't bother to knock on the three golden gates before they speak, and ask themselves if what they're saying is true, needful, and kind."

Celia hadn't considered what she'd said particularly offensive, but now she realized that in so many words she'd called the woman an outright liar.

"As fascinating as John Whittier must be to you two writers," Annie broke in with diplomacy, "I suggest that we discuss Dickens' banquet before we run out of time." Annie took Celia's hand hidden among the sofa pillows and gave it a squeeze, and Lucy looked away, pretending that she hadn't seen the gesture of friendship that had passed between them.

9

The Fields were to host Dickens during his Boston stay, and Celia was thrilled to be at the center of the excitement. After Lucy Larcom had left, Annie confided that they'd already sold $9,000 in tickets—Charles Dickens would return to England a rich man.

"Fortunately, we have seats," Celia said. "Levi told me not a ticket was to be had, even for several hundred desperate Harvard students."

Annie twisted her delicate fingers. "It's those impossible speculators. Dickens' man Dolby was supposed to have stopped it by limiting the number of tickets per person, but it hasn't helped. James is at his wit's end. Mr. Longfellow is at the Tickner Bookshop right now trying to arrange something for those students."

Celia consulted her watch. "I must be going," she said, standing. But Annie took both her hands and gently pulled her back onto the divan.

"Please stay," she pleaded. "You just arrived, and besides, I want you to listen to some of the menus."

"I thought Lucy was going to help do that." They looked at each other and laughed.

"Oh dear, I did too. The woman's unpredictable," Annie said. Her smooth forehead puckered into a frown. "But I can't worry about her. My immediate concern is what to serve at the banquet. Being Christmas time, he's bound to read *A Christmas Carol*, and Mrs. Cratchit's redolent goose will hold such sway in their minds that I'm sure anything I present will seem like stewed prunes. By the way, his mother Kate actually wrote a cookbook. It's called *What Shall We Have For Dinner*. I have it here somewhere."

"Maybe it would give you a clue."

"It gave me a clue all right," Annie said, picking up a small book from the top of her writing tablet and opening it to a yellowed bookmark. "The following is what Mrs. Dickens, alias Lady Maria Clutterbuck, served to eighteen dinner guests. Are you ready?"

Celia nodded.

"She recommends two soups and fishes, and in another menu she suggests carrot soup and turbot with shrimp sauce. After these trifling taste teasers, one is to serve mushroom patties, pork cutlets, oyster curry, and lamb's fry."

"Lamb's fry? What on earth is that?"

"I suppose it's a London specialty." Annie continued: "Grenadine of veal, four quarters of lamb, boiled chicken, tongue, new potatoes, spinach salad, larded capon, and roast pigeon, asparagus, Italian macaroni, rice pudding, Brunswick sausage, and toasted cheese."

"The sausage comes after the pudding?" Celia asked, suddenly aware that she was ravenous.

Annie flipped a page. "I don't think it's a printing error, because in this next menu the anchovies and cheese are served after the pudding, too."

"No wonder Mr. Dickens walks ten miles a day!"

Annie sighed."Well, somehow I'll live up to his great expectations. The banquet's growing by leaps and bounds. What I want to find out from you, now that Lucy is gone, is when you and Levi will be able to meet Charles for a more intimate gathering?" She took out a small daybook and paged through it. "What about dinner on Sunday, January 5th?"

Celia had no need to check a calendar; these days she rarely left the house. "If Levi has any engagements, he'll just have to cancel them, but I'm sure we can make it. Is it formal?"

"Not to the nines," Annie told her, writing in her little book. "By then, I'm sure Mr. Dickens will be longing for his smoking jacket and slippers. It's my guess he'll soon grow tired of the Parker House, and accept our offer to stay here."

A jovial voice boomed from behind them. "If I have anything to say about it, he'll have moved in with us by Christmas." Clad in a Scotch plaid waistcoat, Annie's six-foot husband James towered in the doorway. "How's my favorite poet from the Isles of Shoals?"

"I'm not sure I should take that as a compliment, James, being that I'm the only poet on the Shoals," Celia teased. As he laughed, she realized how fond she was of him. Were it not for James Fields *The Scarlet Letter* might still be stuffed in Hawthorne's desk at the Custom House. Were it not for James, Dickens would not be giving seventy-six readings throughout the United States. And on a much smaller scale, were it not for his enthusiasm for her poems, she never would be able to meet the monthly bills.

"You women look so cozy," he observed, rubbing together his large hands. "I'm sorry we're having such a cold snap. Charles arrives day after tomorrow on the *Cuba* down at the wharf."

"The sun that brief December day rose cheerless over hills of grey," Celia quoted from Whittier's popular poem *Snowbound.*

"The cold is quite enough without snow to complicate matters," he said, and walking over to Annie, placed a hand affectionately on her shoulder. Celia envied them. How happy they looked together.

"Celia and I have been doing some last minute planning and —."

"And I'm afraid I've been little help," Celia broke in. "Cooking for hotel guests is quite different from catering to the eclectic tastes of Charles Dickens."

James offered them a glass of sherry from a crystal decanter, and when they refused, he poured himself a glass."You mustn't hold your talent in such low esteem, Celia. By the way, Mr. Whittier visited us last month and told us all about the Shoals pieces you're writing."

A quiet panic overtook her. She hadn't started them.

"It's an excellent idea," he said. "When you've finished a few, drop them by my office, will you? I might like to publish them as a series in *The Atlantic Monthly.*"

"But James," she protested, "before your enthusiasm leaps out of all proportion, I have to confess that I haven't written one word of the book so far."

He swirled the sherry in the glass and walked to the firescreen. "Now is as good a time as any for the publisher to show his faith in the author's promise. I'm willing to advance you a handsome sum for the series. I've heard your Shoals stories, and I'm sure they're right for us. An advance would allow you more time to write them, wouldn't it?"

"He's right, you know, Celia," Annie said. "You could hire a cook and a girl to lighten the chores. It will benefit both you and James."

"How can I refuse," Celia said, looking from one to the other, "when both of you gang up on me like this?" Still, she had reservations. Telling a story was one thing, writing it, another. Besides, up to now she had written only poems. Could she sit down and write page after page?

James changed the subject, as if to dispel her doubts. "How is Mr. Thaxter? We've heard that he's been ill."

"He's completely recovered," she said, not wanting to dwell on Levi's illness. "But even if he came down with the scarlet fever, pneumonia, and typhoid all at once, I'm sure he wouldn't miss your dinner party for Charles Dickens. I can't thank you and Annie enough for inviting us."

"Ah, you confounded romantic poets," James said and chuckled, "always dreaming of a free meal. Be forewarned, Celia Thaxter. If you haven't told at least one Shoals story before midnight, we'll have to send you into the scullery."

The grey mare clopped at a fast trot over the cobblestones. Levi charged the driver to speed up, and the sound of the whip cracked through the dry January air. Usually, Celia opposed the cruel beating of street animals, but now she was so distracted she didn't say a word.

They were late. They'd left the house at six o'clock for the railroad, and once in Boston, they went to the livery to hire a private opera bus to Tremont Hall. But everyone else had counted on a private bus, and the wait had been interminably long.

She pulled the buffalo robe about her alpalca dress, tucked her fleece-lined gloves farther into her dark heavy mantle, and pulled the hood around her icy cheeks. The anticipation and exhaustive travel were wreaking havoc on her normally strong constitution.

Levi glared out the window at the old driver bundled to his muttonchops in a heavy coat. "I say, good sir," he shouted, puffing into the brisk night, "are you taking us to King's Chapel burial yard or Tremont Hall?"

The coach reeled around a corner into the gas-lighted Common and met with an impasse of street cars and hotel omnibuses, Hansom cabs, six-passenger Landaus, and one or two mail coaches from outlying towns. Tremont Street was blocked its entire length.

Levi opened the carriage door. "Come, come, Celia. We'll get to the reading faster if we walk."

She slipped off the warm robe and placed her hands on Levi's shoulders. He lifted her down with a conspicuous grunt, which she tried to ignore. Levi cut a dashing figure tonight, though his face still was a bit drawn from the illness. He wore a dark wool cloak and white silk cravat, a tall opera hat, and brandished a gnarled walking stick retrieved on one of his lengthy nature jaunts. They were nearly half a mile away, and Celia skipped to catch up with his long strides.

"To think that the line for ticket sales extended a mile," Levi said, breathlessly overtaking other pedestrians. "I hope this is worth it."

"Levi, please," she panted. "Slow down. I have a stitch in my side. Those greasy cod cakes we ate on the train."

Scores of people with the same idea were crowding the boardwalks.

"He won't start until everyone arrives," she said, lurching to avoid two high-spirited young gentlemen engaged in a walking race to see which would reach the entrance first. They both did, and crowded past the ticket takers four abreast with another couple.

Inside the warmth of the foyer, Celia let her hood fall back. She had decided against a bonnet, figuring that no one liked to sit behind a mess of ribbons and bows. Instead, she did up her hair in a crown of braids interwoven with a dark green velvet ribbon embroidered with seed pearls.

Levi checked their capes, the usherette took their tickets. The hall was the largest in Boston, accommodating two thousand five hundred people on the spacious main floor and in the tiers of balconies. A hubbub greeted them as they paraded behind other couples to their seats.

They were none too early. The gas jets were being dimmed by the legion of usherettes. Celia and Levi spotted Annie near the front and slipped into the row. Celia apologized for being late, and with hasty greetings they settled into their seats. Levi sat next to Longfellow, Celia and Annie together. James was busy backstage.

On stage, a large background screen was draped with maroon cloth. A rather spindly reading stand had been placed in front of the screen. Since the cornice gas lights did little to illuminate the front of the auditorium, two tall rods at either side of the lectern supported gas lamps with reflectors. Another series of screens to the side served as stage curtains.

Annie leaned over to Celia. "At this minute, poor Charles is probably taking an egg sherry to soothe his sore throat," she whispered. "He caught a terrible cold in New York."

"He must feel like giving it up."

"James and I tried to convince him he should postpone the reading, but he wouldn't think of it. He's hardly eaten all day."

Celia started to speak, but the audience burst into a sudden uproar at the sight of a man on stage. It was only Dolby, Dickens' right hand man, but the audience gave him an enthusiastic cheer as he turned on the gas lamps. Timidly, the manager darted behind the screen, and once more the undercurrent of excited babble took over.

Annie tapped Celia on the shoulder, and whispered, "Prepare yourself. Here she comes."

Lucy Larcom rushed down a distant aisle and toward them. When she was within talking distance, Celia ventured, "Why, Miss Larcom —." But in her inimitable manner, Lucy dispensed with formalities and got right to the point, addressing everyone and no one. "Have you heard Dickens read before? I heard him last night and he was wonderful. It's simply incredible that he not only writes so well, but reads well, too." She caught sight of a friend across the hall, and bobbed into the air, waving so vigorously that almost everyone between them and her friend focused their attention on her. "Well, I must get back to my companion. It was nice talking with you."

Celia turned slightly and tried to make out the friend Lucy had waved to. John Whittier? She closed her eyes and calmed her frazzled nerves by imagining a sea gull wheeling over Appledore in a clear blue sky. When she opened them, the lights had dimmed, and Charles Dickens stood center stage.

He was an imposing man with a receding hair line that glowed strangely in the bright reflected light. Two tufts of hair stuck out on both sides of a wide part, and he wore a walrus moustache and door-knocker beard that stood out over his black dress cravat. The cravat was adorned with a stick pin set with a brilliant black stone that gleamed in the eerie light of the reflectors. He stood assessing the audience, his hands holding onto the black satin lapels of his black velvet jacket —a gesture at once commanding and imperious. The spectators stilled to a hushed silence.

He placed his gloves and handkerchief on the ledge of the reading stand, and with composure he poured a glass of water. Then in a voice that knew no end to inflection, he began to read. A murmur went up as the audience recognized the opening passage.

> *Whether I shall turn out to be the hero of my own life, or whether that station will be held by anybody else, these pages must show. To begin my life with the beginning of my life, I record that I was born (as I have been informed and believe) on a Friday, at twelve o'clock at night. It was remarked that the clock began to strike, and I began to cry simultaneously.*

10

Celia shifted from one sore foot to another. Her new high button shoes were killing her. Henry Longfellow arrived at the Fields' home just after they did, and thumped Levi good-naturedly on the back. When a cold draft blew into the foyer, the butler quickly closed the door, leading them into the parlor where Annie already was seated with a young man.

"This is Appleton Brown," Annie said, introducing them all. "He's telling me about his new paintings. James is in the library with Charles clearing up a literary wager. Wouldn't you know it?"

"That sounds enticing," Longfellow said, shooting his cuffs and fussing with his bow tie.

"I've never seen you looking so lovely, Annie," Levi said. Annie's silky complection was heightened by the rose sheen of her gown; she glowed.

"My exact words," the young artist piped up.

Annie dismissed the compliments. "Appleton is destined to be another Corot. It's only a matter of time."

"Mrs. Fields is too kind. I do some landscapes. But I'm only starting out."

"Fiddlesticks," Annie disagreed. "You're not just any Sunday painter." She turned to Celia. "You would adore his paintings, especially the apple orchards."

"Do you have an affinity for apple blossoms, Mr. Brown?" Celia asked, sitting down beside the young man.

"How could he help it with the name Appleton, my dear?" Levi quipped. He was so used to his own sarcasm he mistook it for wit.

"We have a few wild apple trees on Appledore, Mr. Brown," she said, trying to make up for her husband's indiscretion. "And I prize those trees more than an entire orchard. Despite the harsh weather we have on the island, each spring the poor little trees inflate in a glory of blossoms. Against the grey of the granite, it's perfection."

"Who is this charming woman speaking prose as though it were poetry?" Charles Dickens' charismatic presence erupted on all of them. He wore the same velvet vest and jacket he'd worn to the reading in addition to a strange huge coat that looked like an exotic Chinese costume.

"This is our island treasure, Celia Laighton Thaxter," James said, winking at her. "They call her Rose of the Isles."

Celia blushed and curbed her protest of the despicable label, because it was in jest. Then James introduced her husband.

"And do you also hail from these mysterious Isles I've been hearing so much about, Mr. Thaxter?" Dickens said, covering a persistent cough with his handkerchief.

"No, only my wife has that distinction." Levi was not smiling.

Searching for something positive to say about Levi's career, Celia clearly was relieved when James came to the rescue.

"Mr. Thaxter is making quite a name for your compatriot Robert Browning here in the States," James said. "Because of Mr. Thaxter's readings of Browning's poems, more copies of the poet's books are sold here than in England."

"How extraordinary!" Dickens exclaimed."So you're also involved in the elocutionary arts."

Levi smiled. "I give a few readings here and there."

But Charles' attention was on Celia and the seashell necklace that rose and fell against her fair skin. When the maid announced dinner, Dickens maneuvered to Celia's side and glanced at Levi. "With your permission, I'd like to accompany Mrs. Thaxter to the table. I'm intrigued by these Isles of hers."

Celia felt as if she'd died and gone to heaven. She passed her hand through the crook of the distinguished author's elbow and entered the dining room. Appleton, Levi, and Henry filed behind the two couples.

Charles drew back her chair and took the seat opposite. Each setting had been marked with individual silk-covered cards inscribed in Annie's fine hand. "Well," their hostess said, "since we're missing three tonight, I propose that the gentlemen sit where they will."

Levi glared at Celia from his cater-corner. He was in an arbitrary mood, and she desperately hoped that Henry Longfellow would cheer him up. Appleton Brown sat on her right, drawing up his chair to restore his view of Annie busy ladling lobster bisque from a Wedgewood tureen. At the same time, the maid removed plates of empty shells, the oysters having been downed in an instant, so deliciously fresh were they.

Dickens set upon his soup before the others were served, and startled by his disregard for their hostess, Celia hesitated, wondering whether she should wait or follow his lead. Suddenly, he looked up, his spoon in mid-air, and promptly set it down again. "I'm terribly sorry," he said. "I felt so at home that I completely forgot and started eating the way we do at home in England."

Annie patted him affectionately. "It's perfectly all right, Charles. James and I remember our own dismay when we were abroad."

"But here I am in the presence of the *bon ton* of Boston."

James laughed and tucked his napkin over the white bib of his dress shirt and collar. "You'll never be assembled with such humble and forgiving *bon ton* as these, Charles." He rapped on the table and proposed a toast to Dickens' health.

Appleton had spoken little. The man seemed self-conscious to the point of speechlessness, and Celia commiserated with him because she too was feeling the pressure of being in the presence of their illustrious guest. She noticed that Levi had polished off his glass of wine and asked the maid for a refill. Longfellow, too. They would be a merry pair by the end of the evening.

"You do have the best fish here in Boston," Dickens said, taking a bite of halibut. "The other day on one of my jaunts I chanced on a pub called the Union Oyster House. It had the best clam chowder I ever ate."

"But you haven't tasted the chowder at our hotel," Celia told him.

Dickens put down his wine glass. "On the Isles of Shoals?"

"Yes, the Isles of Shoals," she repeated in a whisper, a recent habit when she talked of her island home.

"Do I discern a note of sadness in your voice?" Dickens asked, leaning across the table toward her as if they had more in common than this brief dinner. "Tell me about them. Where are they located? What's their history?"

Celia described each of the nine islands that dwindled to seven at low tide: Londoner's named for the London Trading Post, which the Shoalers' quaint speech had transformed into Lunging Island. Duck Island, where her brothers hunted for geese and willet. Smutty-Nose with its colony of Norwegian fishermen. And Star, which had the most inhabitants during the eighteenth century when its shores were crowded with fish drying racks. Dunfish, named for their color, were a primary export from the islands to England. Then, there were Cedar and Malaga Islands, both only a few acres, and White and Seavey Islands where she spent her childhood. Last of all, she described Appledore where she entertained her friends. "John Greenleaf Whittier has been there, and Harriet Beecher Stowe," she said, recognizing in her voice a sense of pride. How could she help but be proud? These were people she admired and respected, and they had accepted her offer to come to her cottage to do their work.

The lines at the corners of Dickens' eyes crinkled toward his close-arched brows. "I spent a summer on the Isle of Wight and left in a worse state than when I arrived," he confessed. "I couldn't get through one page of writing."

Celia laughed. "I assure you that you would work on the Shoals. They're an inspiration."

Annie passed around a platter of roast duck and bright green peas. Dickens refused, handed it to Levi, and said, "I prefer year around at my own place, Gad's Hill, to summer watering holes."

Celia leaned toward him. "But the hotel guests are quite different. At my parlor the artists and musicians and writers really do work. In fact, Appleton, I hope you will join us next summer."

The artist had been listening from the other end of the table and perked up. "It does sound like an artist's paradise."

Annie peered down the table. "Charles, you aren't eating. Could I offer you some cold quail from the pantry? Would that suit you better?"

Dickens shook his head. "Thank you, Annie. I'm still a bit shady."

"If not viand," James added, "perhaps some *vino*, eh, Charles?" He held up a long thin bottle. "Vintage *Lachryma Christi* from our trip to Italy. How about a taste of b*ella Italia*?"

Sighs of contentment followed as the wine was poured and savored. Celia, who usually turned down alcohol, longed for a taste of the golden liquid. Her curiosity whetted, she too held up her wine goblet.

"Aha!" Dickens teased. "I see that we're in the presence of a lady who doesn't allow teetotalism to destroy her prandial pleasures."

She sipped the wine with enjoyment and smiled across the table. Levi and Henry, who had discussed Dante from *The Inferno* to *Paradiso*, suddenly stopped talking to listen to Charles.

"Everyone has proposed a cure for this beastly American cold," Dickens said. "Perhaps you have a traditional Shoals remedy I should hear about, Celia. I've concocted quite a few punch cocktails that would scare the devil, but nothing seems to get rid of this blasted cold. My latest experiment came from my New York landlord who insisted that a Rocky Mountain Sneezer would do the trick and cure me in minutes. So I mixed the potion consisting of brandy, rum, bitters, sugar, and a secret ingredient most rare to these parts, namely, freshly fallen snow."

James laughed between bites, while Appleton forgot his shyness and joined in.

"The landlord," Dickens continued, "deciding I should not drink alone, proposed a toast to my health and together we quaffed the contents of the whole pitcher. He was right. It worked in minutes, but instead of being cured, I was laid out like a stiff at the morgue. I don't think I've yet fully recovered from the prescription."

They slid back their chairs as the maid removed the cruets and sauce bottles, placing them on the sideboard before whisking crumbs off the soiled cloth. As they all resettled, she appeared with a flaming plum pudding crowned with a holly wreath. The blue flames flared as she set it in front of the guest of honor. Dickens threw up his arms in ministerial benediction, the sleeves of his great coat spread like wings in the light of the candelabra. The Charles Street house was so narrow that the rooms were stacked into five stories with the kitchen in the basement. It was no wonder that the maid looked a bit frazzled and weary by the time this last course was served.

More than an hour had passed, and the combination of good wine, food, and company had released them from the tedious decorum required when they first met. James took out a box of cigars and passed them to the men as Annie and Celia retired to the drawing room upstairs. Celia desperately wanted to stay behind. She hoped they wouldn't smoke long. She would pump Levi for every missed word when they got home.

"Annie, your dinner was superb," Celia said, knowing how hard she had worked to make the evening a success. "Did you see how Charles took two helpings of the pudding?"

Annie picked up her needlework and untangled a skein of silk thread from her sewing box. "Yes, but I assure you he's feeling miserable because of that cold. He ate little else." She pulled the needle slowly through the hoop, then paused in mid-air. "I'm worried about him. He's —."

Baffled by Annie's loss for words, Celia let her imagination run wild. Was Dickens seeing another woman? Or in debt? Talk-of-the-town columns claimed that his brother had left a widow and three children without a penny. But more than anyone, Celia knew enough not to rely on those gossip mills.

Annie's voice dropped to a whisper. "Last night I woke up because someone was rattling around in the hall. I caught the maid tiptoeing past, and when I asked what she was doing she said, 'Excuse me, mum, if I disturbed you, but Mr. Dickens was asking after the laudanum.' "

"Is that all? Why should that worry you? I take a dose occasionally myself. And surely you and James must take it once in awhile or you wouldn't have it in the house."

Deep male laughter resounded from the hall and they could hear footsteps in the stairwell. Annie leaned furtively toward Celia and drew her closer. "Yes, I know, a spoonful to calm the nerves, but Celia —." She glanced toward the door, then continued. "The maid took Charles a new full bottle. It was more than half gone when he returned it this morning."

Annie sat upright, picked up her needle, and rapidly drew it through the flower pattern. With nothing to occupy her hands, Celia pretended to gaze into the fire. But her mind sparked with conjecture. Maybe the readings were too much of a strain on Dickens. If she had insomnia but had to read to thousands of people every night, perhaps she too would take large doses of opium. Surely he couldn't be addicted.

The men entered the room and arranged themselves in the arm chairs around the fire. In a feeble voice, Henry, who was getting on in years, filled Annie and Celia in on their conversation. "Charles has told us that he and Dr. Holmes played Scotland Yard this afternoon and went to Harvard to inspect the rooms where Professor Webster murdered, and — forgive me, dear ladies — chopped up the body of Dr. Parkman."

Bostonians still talked about the horrid axe murder as though it had just happened. Rumor had it that Webster stuffed the dismembered corpse of his colleague into a drawer in the chemistry laboratory.

"Do go on," Levi prodded enthusiastically, crossing his legs and waiting with impatience while Longfellow stroked his Rip Van Winkle beard.

Apologetically, Henry looked first toward Celia and then Annie. "I don't think this will offend the ladies. It concerns a party I attended at Webster's a year before the murder. We were still sitting at the dining table sipping our wine. Unlike this esteemed gathering, the guests he'd brought together weren't too compatible.

"Without any warning whatsoever, Dr. Webster snuffed out the candles. Here, I must explain that the weird professor refused to install gas lamps in his house or his laboratory, where surely they would have served much better than candles. In any case, we sat uncomfortably in the dark until the servant was rung for. She entered the room holding a candlestick in one hand and a large bowl in the other. Both Holmes and myself thought she had brought us some punch, and truthfully, at that point we could have used it.

"But the maid set the bowl in front of Dr. Webster, and we quickly discerned that it was not to be drunk. Even a Rocky Mountain Sneezer doesn't glow in the dark."

Dickens chuckled.

"From all appearances this was the professor's latest experiment in chemical spiritualism. Suddenly, one of the ladies screamed and hysterically swore that an apparition was rubbing against her leg. Dr. Webster ordered the maid, who held the only candle, to get on her hands and knees and extricate the family cat from under the table.

"The bowl glowed in a peculiar manner, casting a mysterious greenish light over Dr. Webster's round face. Being uneducated in spiritual seances, I wondered whether I should conjure a spirit or something of that nature. As these thoughts passed through my mind, Dr. Webster's head seemed to be floating in the luminous vapor rising from the bowl. I was seized with a terrible vision, but thought it must be illusion coupled with the power of suggestion. Soon afterward, Webster excused himself and left the room. The servant relighted the candles. Naturally, while he was gone we questioned each other, and to my amazement, everyone in the room had shared my vision of Webster's head with bulging eyes and lolling tongue. One of the ladies, in addition, saw a rope around his neck —or should I say the apparition's neck? As you know, several months later Dr. Webster was hanged to death for the murder of Dr. Parkman. "

Celia cringed. Many of her Shoals tales were based on legend, and Longfellow's story seemed all the more frightening because it was true.

James broke the spell of silence that had descended. "And now Celia's going to tell us about Captain Scott and the maid he left behind on the Isles of Shoals."

Her heart skipped a beat. How could she possibly tell her simple tales in the presence of these renowned storytellers? She took a deep breath and cleared her throat.

"About fifteen years before my family took over the White Island Light, a man from the mainland was on the Shoals convalescing. He boarded with a fishing family on Star Island, and to pass time he wrote in his journal. As the months went by, he began to notice a transformation not only in his physical condition but spiritually as well. 'In the recesses of these eternal rocks,' he wrote, 'with only a cloudless sky above and an ocean before me, I've shaken the fear of death and believe myself immortal.'

"One bright autumn day, the man walked down to the shore, hired a dory and rowed to a promontory on the east side of Appledore Island. He had just pulled the dory onto the beach when he had a disconcerting feeling that he was being watched. Turning around, he saw a woman gazing seaward. She was dressed in a sea cloak and her fair hair streamed about her face in the stiff October breeze.

"Taking her for a native, he decided that she must be waiting for her husband to come in on a fishing boat. So he too watched awhile for a sail on the horizon.

"But when half an hour had passed and no one came, he walked over to her and asked when her husband was due to return. The woman fixed him squarely with sad blue eyes. 'He *will* come again,' she said. Then she seemed to back up and disappear behind the rocks. The man searched each outcrop above the beach but could find no trace of her. As he rowed back across the channel he couldn't get the image of her out of his mind.

"That Sunday he went to church and asked the villagers about her. But none of them remembered having seen the woman fitting his description, and certainly not on Appledore which was sparsely inhabited. They politely suggested that perhaps he'd been there too long and should return to the mainland.

"So haunted was he by the memory of the woman in the sea cloak that he decided to row back to Appledore Island. The fishermen warned him that a storm was blowing up, but he felt strangely compelled to make the crossing. The dory floundered on the high sea and pitched and tossed through the driving rain, and the spit of land where he hoped to find her was completely covered by thick black clouds. Bracing against the wind, he searched every inch of the promontory and was just about to give up when he heard her voice. 'He *will* come again.' Although he had looked there twice, the woman now stood where he'd first seen her. He braced himself to steady against the wind, but noticed as he looked at her that not a fold of her cloak seemed to move. And then, she was gone.

"When the storm abated, he rowed back, and the fisherman who gave him his lodging was waiting for him, worried by his absence. 'You look like you've seen a ghost,' the fisherman commented. Unsure of his faculties, the man denied having seen anything extraordinary. But as they walked back to the cottage, he became emotionally distraught by the thought that he'd regained his health only to lose his mind. He had never approached the fisherman to ask about the woman, fearing that he would be turned out. Now to his surprise, not only did the fisherman listen attentively to his story, but thanked him for sharing his secret. 'You see, I too have seen the woman,' the fisherman said.

"'But who is she?' the man asked.

" 'I can't be certain, but I think she is Captain Scott's mistress,' the fisherman answered. 'They say she was left on Appledore to guard the pirate's buried treasure until he returned.' "

"What a haunting story," Annie said, staring into the firelight.

Levi nodded. "Yes, no matter how many times I've heard it — and I've heard it quite a few — I'm always impressed."

Charles Dickens accompanied Celia down the stairs and stood at her side as the others said good-night. Holding her cloak, he whispered in her ear, "You *will* come again."

11

Spring had arrived. A phoebe wagging its tail landed with its beak full of building materials for a nest perched in a crabapple tree as Celia swung the laundry basket to her hip and went to the line to hang out the wash. She reached for two pieces of paper hidden in her apron pocket. The first was a note from Annie written the day after the dinner party. Celia's damp fingers smudged the ink, but she didn't have to read the note since she knew it by heart: "Dickens came down for breakfast at half past nine. He took his habitual tea, egg, and rasher of bacon. The very first thing he said to me was, 'Mrs. Thaxter certainly caught my fancy. I woke up in the middle of the night thinking of her.' "

She reached into her pocket a second time and brought out a small white calling card. The front was engraved: *John Greenleaf Whittier, Amesbury, Mass.* She had found the calling card on the table in the entry one day after she'd been out. She turned the card over and read the message hastily scrawled on the back: *I hope to see thee in Amesbury before the arbutus blooms. My best to Mr. Thaxter.*

She returned the card to her pocket and vehemently shook out a white tablecloth. Mustard, which Karl had dumped on it during one of his fits, had failed to bleach out. She'd worked on the spot at the washboard until her knuckles were raw. Before long the stain would be a hole, and then she would have to mend it. Their budget wouldn't permit a new cloth. Perhaps she could persuade her mother to give them some of the linen from the hotel.

No poems. No visits. Only house work, and she was sick of it. She kicked the basket heaped with wrung-out clothes and stomped toward the barn.

Their old horse Pachyderm looked up from his oats. "Come Pachy, you beast, we're going for a ride," she told the animal. Levi usually harnessed him, and she realized it might take some coaxing to get the horse away from the feed bin. She slapped his rump and pulled on his halter. "It's too nice to stay indoors. Don't you smell those lilacs?"

Now that she had decided to go someplace and leave the chores behind, she felt much better. The horse bared its teeth as she pushed her thumb into his mouth and forced the bit back over his tongue. "That isn't so bad." She buckled the martingale and pulled the straps through the breast collar. The roan took in wind as she buckled the girth strap. She undid the buckle, braced her arm, and tugged tighter until the horse exhaled and quickly she notched the girth tighter. "No use playing those tricks on me," she told him, attaching the shafts to the harness. "I know them all."

Leading the roan outside and tying him to a hitching ring she asked the horse, "Now is that everything? Wait here until I get back." She ran inside to leave Karl a note.

That year Levi had indulged in a spanking new dark green buggy with gold trim. She rarely drove it, but today a friend of

Levi had picked him up. Celia attached the shafts to the harness and climbed into the driver's seat. She took the reins and slapped them gently against the horse's withers. When he didn't budge, she implored, "Get-up, you beast. No wonder Levi calls you thick skin. Move!" She slapped the reins harder, and the buggy rolled out the barn and down their street. How long would it take to drive to Amesbury? It would be a pleasant ride, but, of course, she couldn't chance it. Karl would be home soon.

The horse clopped over the cobbles, his ears twitching as Celia hummed a tune. The fields were deliciously green, dotted with dandelions and flocks of cow birds. The trapped feeling she had been prey to dissolved as she repeated aloud what John had written: "I hope to see thee in Amesbury before the arbutus blooms."

All at once, for no apparent reason, the old horse decided to stop short in the middle of the road. "You are a willful nag," she lamented, flicking the reins.

A farmer coming from the opposite direction pulled his wagon to a stop. "Need some help?" he shouted.

Embarrassed because she was blocking the road, she pulled the right check rein to force the obstinate animal to the side. "I think I can manage," she said, but under her breath she muttered injurious oaths which, fortunately, the horse took seriously, trotting forward and leaving space for the farmer to pass.

They rode on awhile. Celia really didn't notice where she was headed until she saw they were paralleling the railroad tracks. A train whistled in the distance, and the horse turned skittish. "Calm down, boy, it's only a train." She hated whips, but now she wished she had brought one. Again, the horse stopped stock still. The train whistled behind them, this time much louder.

Pachyderm whinnied a high terrified reply. What did Levi do to get the horse going? She'd never seen him frightened by a train before. And then she upbraided herself for what a fool she'd been. She had forgotten to put blinders on. The steam engine bore down upon them. Should she jump out and try to lead the shying horse away from the tracks?

The engineer waved as the giant wheels of the engine ground past with deafening noise. But there was no time for waving back. Pachyderm's eye-balls rolled in fear as the engine roared past, and before she could do anything, he bolted. The buggy shot forward, leaving Celia hanging onto the dash. Springs creaked and the hickory wheels jounced in and out the deep muddy ruts of the road. She gripped the check reins with one hand, the edge of the driver's seat with the other, engulfed in a cloud of steam.

"Whoa, Pachy! Whoa boy!" she yelled over the clattering train wheels. The muscles in her arms ached, her fingers burned from the pull of the leather reins.

Passengers strained against the windows of the coach and one of them leaned dangerously out the window shouting over the rumble of the wheels, "Jerk the reins! Jerk hard on the left check rein!"

The runaway horse didn't respond to these or any directions, but set a course of his own. To her horror, the carriage veered recklessly close to the tracks. She peered down at the road on the other side to see if she could jump out. The road was a blur. She clutched the reins to her as the vehicle tipped on two wheel rims, flinging her to the far side of the seat. The horse galloped at top speed, his nostrils flaring, his flanks lathered with foam. Dear God, she prayed, closing her eyes.

When the horse finally tired and slowed to a trot, all she could see of the train was the caboose disappearing over the horizon. "Good Pachy. Easy boy," she whispered. She jerked the curb bit, and the foam-spattered horse neighed softly as Celia clambered out, her knees shaking. She put her arms around his damp neck, burying her face in his mane.

The following week Celia told Levi that she needed a rest and would be going to the Shoals to visit her mother. She did not tell him she also would be visiting John on the way. Karl was the only snag in her plans. She had always taken him with her to the Shoals, and now he couldn't understand why she was leaving him behind. "I'll take you this summer," she promised, trying to ignore his tear-stained face. "Mother might visit a friend on the way."

Why should she feel guilty? She would pay John Whittier only a social call. It was all quite proper. All quite above reproach. If she were to catch the last boat to the Shoals, she had to leave his house no later than three in the afternoon.

Levi drove her to the depot, and on the way he said, "Karl told me you're going to visit a friend on the way to the Shoals."

"Yes, I did tell him that." She paused longer than she wanted. "I made it up so Karl wouldn't feel badly about being left behind."

Levi scrutinized her with narrowing eyes. "And why aren't you taking him this time? God knows you're the only one who can handle him."

Struck by a pang of anxiety, she stared at her husband. If he ever found out, would he be jealous? Of course, he would, because he was jealous even of Karl and her mother. With all the confidence she could muster, she faced him. "I want to be alone for awhile. That's all. Don't worry. I've left instructions with the maid so you needn't worry about Karl."

When the train pulled into the station Celia made her way to the ticket office. She shoved the money through the window and lowered her voice. "I'd like a ticket to Amesbury, please."

"Have to speak up, Ma'am. Can't hear you," the grey-haired clerk said, leaning forward and putting his hand to his ear.

A line was forming behind her. She looked around to see if Levi could overhear, but he was at the door waving for her to hurry. "Amesbury," she said louder, pushing her face close to the window.

"Amesbury," he repeated loudly. She stuffed the ticket into her purse and hurried toward her waiting husband.

"What took you so long?" Levi snapped. "The train's about to leave."

"I think the ticket seller was stone deaf. Levi, dear, you go on. I can board myself," she said, realizing that the conductor would have to punch her ticket and might call out her destination as she boarded.

Levi swung her valise up the steps. "Don't be silly. I may be a wretched husband, but nobody ever accused me of not being a gentleman."

Fortunately, the conductor was nowhere in sight. She followed Levi into the coach and took a window seat while he placed her valise overhead and slid her Gladstone bag beneath the seat.

"You won't stay longer than a week," he stated categorically.

"I have to see how Mother is. If she's feeling poorly, I might stay longer." Celia removed her bonnet and held it on her lap.

Levi picked up her hand and twisted the seashell bracelet around her wrist once. "The last time I saw you wear this was at Mr. Dickens' dinner party. What's the special occasion now? Is it because you're getting away from me?"

She drew back her wrist, trying not to sound upset. "Levi, you must get off or you'll be going with me."

He turned to leave and bumped into the conductor. "We're pulling out in two minutes flat," the conductor warned. "May I see your tickets, please?"

Celia fumbled through her purse.

Levi stepped in front of the conductor. "I'm saying good-bye to my wife."

Clutching her ticket, she pulled away as Levi's lips pressed hard against hers.

"Thank you," he told the bewildered conductor. "Look out for her until she gets to Portsmouth, will you?" He turned and strode back down the aisle.

The conductor took Celia's ticket and stopped before punching it. "Says here you're going to Amesbury, Ma'am. Didn't you want a through ticket to Portsmouth?"

"No, that won't be necessary. Eventually, I am going to Portsmouth, but I'm visiting friends first," she explained, retrieving the deceptive ticket and tucking it safely out of sight.

12

Before she'd left that morning Celia had referred to a list of flower sentiments. Arbutus was said to express, "Thee only do I love." She smiled, thinking that just last year she had sent John scarlet geraniums, which, according to the same little book, stood for "Silliness."

As she recalled John's handsome broad forehead and penetrating eyes, excitement filled her with warm and daring anticipation. She took out a small mirror, arranged her hair, powdered her nose, and made sure she didn't have any smudges of train soot on her face.

The hansom rattled to a standstill before a low white house with green shutters and a vine-covered piazza on one side. She asked the driver to wait, and stepped onto the curb. Conveniently for the Quaker poet, the Friends Meeting House was across the street.

But standing on the threshold, she was overcome by misgivings. John had no advance knowledge of her visit, and perhaps he was already entertaining someone. One objection after another ran through her mind, and she was about to give up and leave as quickly as she had arrived when a dark curly head stuck out the front door. A matronly woman wiped dripping hands on her apron and, examining Celia, asked, "Yes?" as if addressing a beggar.

"I've come to see Mr. Whittier," she said, handing the woman her calling card.

"Well, y'ain't come to see me, now have you?" the woman replied, dimples appearing in her rosy cheeks. "Sure and I believe Mr. Whittier just stepped out half an hour ago, but I'll be checking the garden room."

She disappeared into the dark house while Celia nodded to the hansom driver, holding up her hand as a signal for him to wait.

"I'm sorry, Missus, but Mr. Whittier isn't t'home," the woman said. "Would you be caring to wait?" She took the calling card embossed *Mrs. Celia Laighton Thaxter* and dropped it into a basket on the foyer table.

"No, I don't believe so," Celia said in a whisper of disappointment.

"And why not? Mr. Whittier would wait forever to see thee."

At the sound of John's voice she whirled around. He stood on the step below so that she looked directly into his eyes. "John Whittier," she said, scolding, "you shouldn't come up behind people like that."

"Kate here was to tell visitors I was out, but surely not thee."

"On the Shoals that would be called a fib, John," she said, distinctly aware that she herself had told her share that day.

John paid the hansom driver, then ushered her into the house. She followed him through the low-ceilinged dining room into a small book-lined room. "This is my study," he announced, throwing open French doors that gave onto a garden. He gently placed his hand on her back as he guided her beneath a dappled grape arbor. "Of course, I can't compete with thy green thumb, Celia, but I do enjoy this bower."

They walked behind the squat, two-story house to a pear orchard in blossom. As they strolled, she paid attention to the rhythm of his step beside hers, and the timbre of his voice, knowing that their memory would prove a solace later on.

"I'd hoped to convince thee to stay with me a few days. I want to talk with thee about thy writing."

She'd never dreamed he would ask her to stay overnight, and she might have acquiesced if his sister Lizzie had been around. But the housekeeper — whoever she was — certainly didn't fill the position of chaperone. Lucy Larcom could carry on like an uninhibited fool, but she could not.

"I'm on my way to the Isles," she said, hoping he wouldn't see through her thin pretext. "Mother's expecting me," she added to further convince him.

John's face clouded with a frown. "I was afraid of thy refusal." Then he brightened. "But I do expect thee for supper." In his study, John rang the service bell and the woman with the disheveled hair reappeared. "Kate, this is Mrs. Thaxter. She's an admirable poet, and she's agreed to dine with me."

Dimples returned to Kate's ruddy cheeks as she curtsied. "Pleased to meet you, Mum. Mr. Whittier has told me so much about you and how 'quisitely you write."

He smiled. "See, Celia. Thou art well-liked in Amesbury. Kate will show thee to Lizzie's room to freshen up."

"Lizzie?"

"Yes, Lizzie my niece. She's moved in and is housekeeping for me these days. Kate here does the washing and prepares my meals when Lizzie is out." Suddenly, John reddened. "Why I never would have asked thee to stay, Celia, without — ."

She raised a hand. "You needn't explain, John. I understand, and I'm so glad that you have someone to look after you," she said almost wistfully, and for a lingering moment they stared at each other, regretting the misunderstanding that had thwarted their real desires.

Celia followed Kate's lopsided apron bow up the steep back flight of stairs to a large bedroom overlooking the street. The train ride had been hot and dusty, and though their reunion had been joyous, she was feeling the strain of the last few minutes. More than ever, she realized she and John weren't merely two poets who had met to talk over their work.

She examined herself in the oak leaf mirror and sighed. Her hair was in complete disarray. She removed her dress and shoes, standing bare-footed on the braided rug and assessed her figure. Although only thirty-three, the birth of her three sons had taken its toll.

Kate returned with a pitcher of hot water, but seeing Celia in her undergarments, hurried away.

Celia ran a damp cloth over her fair skin above the bust line of her corset, and flushed a prickly pink as she remembered Levi's defiant parting kiss on the train. It had been more like the possessive mark of a branding iron than a sign of affection. He had wanted to humiliate her in front of the conductor, and the very thought of his hypocrisy filled her with contempt. She rubbed the cloth over her lips.

Unbraiding her hair and slowly running a brush through it, she let it fall in waves over her bare shoulders, and for a moment she wished John could see her, standing behind her looking into the mirror.

Quickly she shook out her traveling dress, slipped it back over her head, and rewound her hair. There. She was ready. An oil painting on the papered wall caught her eye. It had a pleasant amateurish style. She pulled back a curtain from the window to read the signature —L. Larcom! A wave of jealousy flared inside her. No doubt Miss Lucy Larcom had stayed overnight in this very room.

On her way down the dark narrow stairs, she hesitated on the last step to imagine what it would be like living with John.

"Is the guest room made up, Kate?" she overheard him say. "Mrs. Thaxter probably will be staying over a few nights."

So that was his plan. Well, she wouldn't allow herself to fall for his guile. Let Lucy cater to his celibate fantasies! John sat on a settee near the open door of his study, a bantam rooster perched on his shoulder. Although Celia had promised herself to be cold and distant, it was impossible with him there stroking a cocky russet bird.

"He's not quite as fun as my old parrot Charlie," he told her. "Charlie used to climb the lightning rod and call 'Whoa!' to horses in the street."

Despite her best intentions, Celia laughed, and described her experience with the runaway horse.

"And what did thy husband say when the carriage returned? Was he not vexed with thee putting thy life in danger like that? If I were thy husband I'd —."

"I didn't tell him," she confessed as the rooster pecked at her fingers.

"I'd give thee a sound Quaker reprisal."

"And what would that be?" she asked, enjoying his feigned rebuke.

"One whole week of silence," he said, stretching out his finger as a perch for the rooster. "But I daresay, thou would have thy own way, and we would have to make do with but a few minutes."

She smiled. So he too was thinking what it would be like if they lived together.

After lunch they returned to his study and she admitted that she found little time to work on the Shoals essays for *The Atlantic Monthly.* She talked about Levi's illness, and Karl's tantrums. "Sometimes I'm in the middle of a poem and I have to leave it mid-stanza to make Karl stop screaming."

John listened gravely, sitting beneath the calm scrutiny of a bust of Marcus Aurelius. He rocked back in his chair, his eyes half-closed. "I've kept every one of thy letters from the Shoals, Celia," he said, opening his eyes to look at her. "Perhaps I could let thee use them as a reference."

She studied him as he spoke. Even now, relaxed as he was, he magnetized her.

"It's thy destiny to write a prose work about the Isles, and I have no doubt concerning thy talent." He rocked forward and rummaged in the cubbyholes of his desk until he found some letters. He searched methodically through them and handed her a small folded sheet of paper. "Take this. I wrote it for thee."

She took the paper, starting to unfold it. But John gently placed his hand on hers —she must wait to read it. The touch of his hand raced through her entire body, and he too must have felt the same surge of excitement because he immediately withdrew it.

"Read this when thou art in need of encouragement, sweet Celia," he said softly.

Kate came barging into the room and apologized. "Sorry, Mr. Whittier, but I come to say I've washed up and will be going now.

Should I come Monday or will you be wanting me sooner?" She cast a curious glance at Celia.

"Not unless Mrs. Thaxter has changed her mind about staying," he said, betraying neither hope nor discouragement. But his eyes implored her to relent.

"If I hurry, John, I'll make the last steamer for the Shoals."

"Well, then," Kate said, backing toward the door, "I'll be on my way, too."

"Is this a conspiracy?" John asked with sudden mock levity. "Shame for abandoning a poor old bachelor."

Ten minutes passed before John could find her a cab, and another ten before she arranged herself in the corner of the train compartment.

Finally settled, she opened her purse and took out the sheet of paper, turning it over and over, desperately wanting to read it. But she knew this wasn't the time or the place. He'd asked that she read the letter when she was discouraged, and certainly she needed no encouragement today. For she was sitting on top of the world, and John had put her there.

Murder

13

Appledore in winter was hardly cheerful. The bathing pool looked sadly deserted. The boats were stowed away. Even the wharf had been towed onto dry land. Dozens of piazza rocking chairs filled the Laighton cottage, and the closed off dining room was draped with tarps and sails. The main hotel windows had been boarded over and shuttered fast against harsh winter storms.

When the doctor ordered Levi to a warmer climate, he took John and Roland with him to Florida. Celia rented out the large Newtonville house and went to the Shoals to be with her mother. For the first time since her marriage, she had more than enough time to work on her writing. Her first book of poems, a small collection, was published in 1871. Surprisingly, Levi paid for it—no doubt in retribution for having deserted her.

John Whittier wrote Celia on Appledore reminding her about the Shoals book, but somehow she couldn't get started. She sat at her desk with every intention of writing the first paragraph, labored on one sentence for hours, but at day's end, threw her efforts into the waste-paper basket. It was difficult for her to imagine how this bleak island existence could possibly appeal to sophisticated Boston society.

One evening they huddled around the cook stove in the kitchen. Karl and Celia's mother were playing a game of bezique. The copper kettle whistled softly, and she got up to make them some tea, passing behind Karl so that she could help him with his cards. When no one came to his rescue he was known to deliberate a painfully long time.

"No fair, Celia," her mother said. "Can't you see he's winning already."

She patted her son on the back. "Karl, you're getting to be a real card shark. If you were playing for filthy lucre, we'd all be rich."

Karl beamed. His hair was tousled and one suspender hung carelessly off a shoulder.

Karen Christensen came into the kitchen, warmed her hands over the stove, and stuck another log into the firebox. She had never married. At first she lived with her sister Maren on Smutty-Nose, but then Celia's mother took her into service, and gradually taught her a few words of English.

Celia never had seen her wear anything but a royal blue muslin dress which she'd woven herself, in addition to a starched white apron and linen collar. Tonight, Celia stole long glances at Karen as she sat in the lamplight humming a Norwegian song. "And how are Anethe and Ivan getting along now that they're married?" she asked.

"They is doing very well, Mrs. Thaxter," Karen said. "I teach them some English, too." She got up and poured hot water into the tea pot.

"How wonderful to have the family all together," Celia said with a tinge of envy, thinking of her own scattered family. "Maren must be so happy."

"Oh, yes, Mrs. Thaxter. And my brother's wife Anethe, she is a wonderful girl. I like her much."

Karl looked up from his cards. "I want to spend Christmas with you!" he shouted.

"Why, Karl," Celia said. "I know you're fond of the Christensens, but don't you want to be with Gram and me on Christmas day?" She exchanged a troubled look with her mother. The boy was unfathomable.

"I don't. I don't!"

Embarrassed by his sudden outburst, Celia laughed nervously. "See what a spell your family has over my son, Karen?"

Karen poured their tea and went to her spinning wheel in the corner. The treadle squeaked rhythmically as she wound a spool of worsted yarn.

Karl glared at the cards. All of a sudden, he scooped them up and flung them into the air. A King and Ace landed in Celia's lap and several of them fell onto the stove. Quickly, Celia's mother grabbed a pot holder and whisked them onto the floor.

"Karl, what am I going to do with you?" Celia's voice rose in desperation. "Will you ever learn to curb your temper? We don't always get what we want. Now apologize this minute and go straight to your room. Is this any way to act in front of Karen?"

Karl's mouth skewed into an ugly grimace. When he was younger, Celia had been able to appease him, but now, as he towered beside her with his hands clinched into fists, she feared his violent outbursts.

"Apologize," she ordered again.

"All right. I'm sorry. Sorry. I'm sorry!" he screamed, his face turning red.

Celia pushed him forcefully into his chair and held a tea cup to his lips. She had been through this enough times to know that it only hindered her when she showed how upset she was.

"Mother, will you get the laudanum?" Eliza Laighton hobbled over to the cupboard, took down a bottle, and measured a tablespoon.

Karl pursed his lips so tightly they turned blue. "Come on, my poor little spud," Celia begged. "Take this for my sake. It'll make you feel much better." His eyelids drooped.

Karen approached the table, knelt beside Karl, and looked into his face with her calm grey eyes. "I tell you what, Karl. When spring come , we all go on a bignig in the boat. You and Anethe and me. All right?"

The Norwegians had a way with Karl. Perhaps it was because of their broken English and innocent, untroubled acceptance of life from day to day.

While Karen held Karl's attention, Celia forced the spoon into Karl's mouth. He cried out as if betrayed, and most of the amber liquid dribbled over his young beard. Experience had taught her to give him twice the recommended dose because much of it never reached his mouth.

With head lowered to his hands, Karl sobbed as though his heart were broken. The opium took effect almost immediately. If they didn't get him to bed, he would have to sleep in the kitchen all night. Her brothers had gone visiting and probably wouldn't be home until midnight.

"Come, Karl, let's get you into bed. We have a long day ahead of us."

He slumped forward, his head on the table. Karen stood to one side of him, Celia on the other, and together they hefted him onto his feet.

"Come now, dearest," she urged. "Make an effort. I know you're groggy, but try to help Mother."

Her despondent son stumbled toward the downstairs parlor. In winter they blocked off the upstairs and lived in the rooms downstairs. With joint effort, she and Karen pushed, dragged, and shoved Karl toward his bed near the parlor stove. Celia unwound the laces of his boots and loosened them through the grommets. Karen took hold of one boot, Celia the other. Karen pulled so hard that she ended up on the other side of the room head over heels.

"Are you all right?" Celia asked, giggling as she picked Karen off the floor.

"You have very patience, Mrs. Thaxter."

"I need to," she said smiling at the cryptic compliment and covering her son with a blanket.

They returned to the kitchen where her mother was on her hands and knees picking up what remained of the bezique cards. Eliza Laighton swiped her grey hair from her forehead. "I was so worried, Celia. When he's like that I worry what he'll do next."

Celia did too, but now wasn't the time to say so. "He's sleeping like an angel, Mother. He just doesn't have control over his emotions. You have to think of him as a perpetual twelve-year-old."

"But he's getting so big," Eliza argued. "Someday he's going to hurt himself or someone else with that temper of his."

They had been over what to do with Karl a hundred times, and each member of her family thought they had the right solution. Levi's was to avoid him. Her mother's was to worry to death. Her brothers' was to treat Karl as though he were a normal rational being. Pretending that Karl was like everyone else worked best, although at times such as this, the pretense was futile. Only one solution existed for Celia, and that was to love him and patiently try to help him through the worst of it. But was this the worst? Could his poor addled mind lead him to a destruction beyond the realm of her compassion and understanding?

Karen sipped tea, staring into her cup. Last summer Celia had written a poem about her. Actually, she had composed it at a church service on Star Island. That Sunday lingered in her memory for a number of reasons, the prime one being that John had come to the Shoals for a long week-end, and he'd accompanied her to the stone chapel.

It was one of those bright blue and sunny days, and the chapel bell pealed over the waves. Debonair as always, John doffed his top hat and held out his hand to help her from the boat. She was expert at getting in and out, even with half a dozen petticoats on, but her brother Oscar, who appreciated the art of matchmaking, suddenly rocked the boat, sending her headlong into Whittier's arms. Celia chided them, but she wasn't really upset. Star Islanders cared little about reputations, and such harmless flirtation would go unnoticed on an island where marriage was as suspect as taxes.

They filed down the aisle of the chapel and into a middle pew. The small congregation was composed mostly of women, their men being at sea. The rough-hewn pew in front of them was scratched with the initials of restless children. The inside Indian shutters were half-closed to discourage day dreaming during the sermon, but the slit of blue sky all the more distracted Celia. With John beside her, she could concentrate on little except his broad shoulder touching hers. The pastor's black robe swept down the aisle. And then a group of Norwegians entered the pews on the side opposite Celia.

John and Maren Hontvet were there with Maren's sister Karen, who sat next to someone Celia didn't recognize.

The stranger occupied Celia's thoughts during most of the sermon. His hair was dark and wavy and he wore a trim Van Dyke beard. He was handsome, and she wondered if Karen were sweet on him. As the last Amen was sung, Celia's brothers bounded from the pew like wild horses. Gallantly, John stepped out and let her pass in front of him. She purposely modulated her step to fall in with Karen and the stranger.

The man seemed overly solicitous as Karen introduced him. "Mrs. Thaxter, I wish you to make the acquaintance of Louis Wagner who stay with us. We look him until he better."

"And what is ailing you, Mr. Wagner?" Celia asked. "Nothing serious, I hope."

The man surveyed her with suspicion. He looked down. "I have rheumatism."

"How dreadful. My husband has rheumatism, and the doctor has recommended a warm climate. Next winter Mr. Thaxter will be in Florida."

Louis Wagner scowled, but didn't look up. "He's fortunate. I can barely afford to go to Boston."

As she talked, he seemed to look right past her. And when he talked, his eyes shifted to her throat or mouth, never her eyes. He spoke with an accent she couldn't place. "Are you from Norway, Mr. Wagner?"

His dark eyes flashed distractedly past her. "I'm an American!" he said with annoyance, drawing Karen away as though he were in a hurry to depart.

As Celia remembered watching them leave, she couldn't help thinking how lonely the women must be when their husbands were fishing.

Suddenly, a shutter banged against the cottage and Celia looked up to see Karen spinning and her mother fast asleep in her rocking chair. Sleet blew against the clapboards, and the wind howled around the northeast corner. "Is Louis Wagner still living on Smutty-Nose?" Celia asked Karen.

"Mr. Wagner leaves weeks ago. We offer him to fish but he stay in Portsmouth with our friend Mrs. Johnson."

"I see." Celia felt strangely relieved. There had been a secretive quality about the man that made her uneasy. "I hope he paid Maren room and board," she added.

"Oh, yes. Louis pay us," Karen assured her.

The Norwegians were poverty stricken. Last summer Celia had asked her friend Ole Bull to give a benefit violin concert at the hotel to help out the fishermen. They were too proud to accept outright charity, but since Ole was Norwegian, too, they let him help.

The spinning wheel creaked awhile. "Louis good man. I never see him drink."

Well, that 's one good thing in his favor, Celia thought. She had just been writing about a man from Star Island who lived alone and had consumed forty gallons of rum in one year.

Karen yawned. "I go bed, Mrs. Thaxter." She stood and kissed Celia fondly on the temple. "I pretend Karl my son. I wear same shoes as you because I love him."

Deeply affected by these words, Celia meant to give Karen a copy of the poem she'd written about her. But she procrastinated, and the following spring when she did remember, it was too late. Karen was dead.

14

The Captain tipped his cap to her as a deck hand stowed their luggage and boxes below. This trip Celia had purchased too many mainland treasures: dry goods and notions for her mother, new works by her friends Sarah Orne Jewett and Henry Dana, as well as beakers, chemicals and plates for Karl's darkroom.

"She's rough today, Mrs. Thaxter," the deck hand said, returning from the bowels of the pack boat. "I think you'd be warmer and safer in the cabin."

The boat swayed and pitched, and Celia hurried Karl down the flight of narrow stairs to the cabin where the air was close and musty. This vessel had none of the grace or swiftness of the Appledore steamer. It ploughed methodically through the whitecaps like a work horse, belching and creaking as it bucked the eight-foot swells. Looking green at the gills, Karl sank down on a carton while Celia snuggled into a worn leather seat near the porthole.

The fog thickened by the minute. Maybe they'd have to put back. A sudden swell pushed her against the varnished cabin wall. Karl moaned, holding onto the crate as the hull creaked beneath them. Somewhere in the distance she heard the muffled clang of a bell buoy. They must be passing Pull and Be Damned Point nearing the mouth of the Piscataqua River.

The deck hand lurched down the stairs dripping rain. "Quite a squall out there, Mrs. Thaxter," he said. "Captain wanted to know if you were all right. I can have the cook make you up some grog if you're cold."

She shook her head. They'd eaten at the steamer restaurant near the pier, and the taste of the two ship-wrecked eggs and pickled beets advertised as "soaked bums" had left them both queasy. The cabin boy lighted a whale oil lamp and set off again to battle the elements.

"Let's play a game, Karl. Can you name the boats we've had at Appledore?"

Karl lurched to the safety of his mother's side and huddled next to her. He thought awhile. "*Celia,*" he said. The boat had been a sixty-ton yacht that could pick up speed when you had a good head wind. The new steamboat was much more reliable and the Laightons had been inordinately proud of the steamer. But to their disappointment *The Boston Journal* reporter had described it as "a rusty black-boilered tub."

"What about the sailing craft?" she asked, taking her son's mind off the rolling beneath them. She waited while he hemmed and hawed. "Don't you remember *Star of the East* and *Factory Girl*?"

The whale light glanced off the fluted tin reflector, flickering over the canvas mail bags and crates piled along the walls. The engine shuddered and the plank floor tipped to a thirty degree angle along with Celia's stomach. If she didn't get some air soon, she was going to be sick. The lock on the porthole was painted fast.

"Come, Karl," she urged, pushing him toward the door. "We have to get on deck where there's some air." She held his clammy hand, helping him up the stairs.

The rain blew horizontally into their faces, but the salty gusts revived them both. They hugged each other cradled in the windbreak of the lifeboat until she sighted the beam from the White Island Light. Never was she so glad to be home.

Cedric and Oscar built a blazing fire in the parlor stove for them to dry out. They decided to eat near the fire, and mimicking some of the more awkward hotel waitresses they'd hired over the years, her brothers paraded in and out carrying bowls of brothy clam chowder and island duck, which her mother had stuffed with cornbread and sausage.

The storm raged for five days, cooping them inside when they longed for spring.

While Celia was away, Karen had decided to find work as a seamstress in Boston. She wondered what had possessed the girl to leave them, but she was even more concerned by what possessed Karl. He kept saying that Karen had promised to take them on a picnic. He called her a liar, and vowed that he'd get even. Celia tried to explain, but Karl had a one-track mind and for some odd reason that track centered on Karen's promise. She tried to distract her son, but he couldn't go outside, and his attention span wouldn't allow him to read a book.

At Christmas his brothers had given him a small diary, which caused them great amusement since Karl's writing ability fell somewhere between a fourth and fifth grader's. So one morning when Celia found Karl curled in an armchair and chewing the end of a pencil, she was surprised. "That diary looks much too small. Do you want a bigger sheet of paper?" she asked, furious at John and Roland for playing such a cruel joke on their brother.

Karl's hand clamped down on what he'd written, and he glowered at her.

"All right, then. Mommy won't look," she said, pleased that at last he was occupied. She turned back to the seeds she was planting. Three mornings in a row they'd eaten boiled eggs so that she could use the halved shells for germinating seeds. She patted down the soil and balanced the shells in a carton on the window sill. There. Ready for spring.

But where was it? Usually by March the boats were scraped, painted, and in the water. Karl squirmed, fiddled, and fussed until Celia could stand it no longer. "Why don't you go see what Uncle Oscar is doing?" she suggested. "Mother wants to concentrate on her writing."

Karl whined, "I want to go on a picnic."

She laughed. "Karl, just take a look out the window. Do you really want to go for a picnic in a blizzard? Be sensible just for once."

The diary fell from his lap and he made no effort to pick it up. He gouged his fists into his eyes. "I want to see Karen," he bawled. "Why won't you take me? You hate me. Karen hates me!"

That settled it. She'd had enough. He was too large for a spanking or she would have lambasted him. With a firm hand she dragged him out of the room and into the kitchen where her mother was knitting. "I beseech you, Mother. Can you find something for Karl to do? He's driving me crazy, and I want to rework the preface on my Shoals piece before I send it off."

Eliza Laighton put down her knitting and smiled at Karl as only a grandmother could. "Run along, Celia. I'll keep him out of mischief."

Relieved, she went back to her room and settled at her desk. She was reading the preface for the third time when her mother called, "Celia, it's Karl!"

She rushed into the kitchen but Karl was nowhere in sight.

The door stood wide open, and her mother was on the porch with thick snow falling on her shoulders. A blast of cold air hit Celia as she ran to her mother's side. Against the stark snowy landscape, she saw Karl bundled in a wool coat spinning like a dervish around the yard.

"It's all my fault," her mother sputtered into her handkerchief. "I asked him to collect some firewood."

With a dull glint in wide menacing circles around Karl's head, an axe gyrated like a lighthouse beacon.

"Oh, dear God!" Celia covered her mouth with a hand. If his bad leg were to give out, Karl could land on the blade.

Her mother was hysterical.

"How long has he been doing this?"

Eliza pulled a wool shawl tightly around her. "I don't know — a few minutes."

Feeling helpless, Celia stared at her son whirling like a faceless phantom. She shivered in the cold, reluctant to leave him out of her sight. Slowly, Karl unwound like a music box figure coming to a halt.

"He'll be all right," she called over her shoulder as she trudged through deep drifts toward him. But suddenly she heard a ringing sound, and froze in her tracks. The axe flew through the air, crashed, and stuck in the side of the shed. As he let it fly, Karl crumpled into the snow.

Celia plunged through the heavy drifts and helped him up.

"Karl, you could have hurt yourself!" she scolded, waving for her mother to go back inside. "Or me," she added, struck by the impact of what he'd done. But from experience, she knew that Karl would neither explain nor apologize. Instead, he would sulk. Well, this time he could sulk alone — and without supper.

15

"March 6, 1873," Celia wrote on an overdue reply to a rambling letter by a would-be poet, who wanted nothing less than a twelve-page treatise on *ars poetica*. Really, if the woman wanted to write, why didn't she just sit down and do it?

She glanced at the clock on the mantle —7:30. They would be stirring downstairs now, and her solitary vigil soon would be over. She pulled a wool lap robe over her knees to ward off the morning chill. Workmen already were hammering over on Star Island. They were building a new hotel, and she hoped the competition wouldn't draw regular guests from Appledore.

She stared out the window. Gulls soared through the silvery morning light, their outspread wings diaphanous against the sun. Wasn't that Carpenter Ingebretsen tromping through the snow past her window? He was heading at a fast clip straight for the servants' quarters. No doubt he'd find them all asleep. They were a lazy bunch these days.

"March 6, 1873," Celia wrote at the upper right corner of another sheet. She resented the time this petty correspondence took away from her own writing and wondered how John managed to keep up with his fan mail.

Ingebretsen reappeared accompanied by some Norwegian workmen her brothers had hired to help open the hotel. What was going on? The men were carrying shotguns, their strides long and determined. She rushed to her door and called down the hall. "What's happening?"

Her mother called back in a hoarse sleepy voice, "Something about Smutty-Nose."

Celia went back to her desk. Probably a drunk. Or some poor soul who hadn't voted the way the Shoalers thought he should so they decided to hove 'em up again' the meetin' hus to make him see their way. It wouldn't be the first time. But wasn't it early for politics? All of a sudden one of the servants, still in her nightdress, came running from the back shouting. Another girl followed. Celia shoved up the window.

"Karen's dead! Anethe's dead!" they screamed.

She slammed down the window, wanting to believe it was one of her brothers' practical jokes. But when a wailing reached her from the kitchen below, she plummeted down the hall and swung open the kitchen door.

The fishermen and servants lined the walls and were talking all at once.

"We search Appledore," a Norwegian workman said. "He might be here."

"Ya. Is good idea. I think so, too," another agreed.

Eliza Laighton was weeping. "Now, Mother," Cedric comforted. "Karen left us. It was her idea. You can't blame yourself." Then, realizing that Celia was standing there and hadn't been informed what was happening, he motioned to the others for silence.

Blinking back his tears, Carpenter Ingebretsen walked up to Celia. "Karen is dead. Anethe is dead. Louis Wagner killed them. Maren say so. She half crazy." The muscles over his high cheekbones twitched in anger. "We go find him."

One thing Karl had taught Celia was how necessary it was for her to curb her emotions during traumatic situations, and act instead. Without hesitation, she assured the old man that she would go to Maren immediately to see if she was all right.

Her mother looked up from puffy lids. "Celia, you must be careful. The man is dangerous and he could be anywhere on the island."

Oscar stepped forward. "I'll take her to Maren's and then I'll join the search."

"Let me go too," a new girl named Ida offered.

Ingebretsen's son Waldemar motioned for the men to follow him outside, and yelling for revenge, they gathered on the porch. When Cedric walked toward the door to join them, Celia begged him to stay. "Please! What if Wagner's on Appledore? Mother will be here without any protection."

Ida stepped forward. "I know how to shoot, Mrs. Thaxter," she said, boldly eyeing the rifle over the fireplace. Cedric took down the Winchester and loaded it. He handed it to the girl, and before Celia could protest further, he'd joined the others.

She sat down and pulled on an old pair of oil boots.

"I remember when we were all sitting here together," her mother said, "you and Karen and Karl —." Her voice trailed into sad silence.

Karl! How could Celia have forgotten him? She tugged at her brother's sleeve. "I have to see if Karl's all right." She ran down the hall to Karl's room, tripping on the carpet runner and catching at the wall for support.

"Karl, wake up!" Her pulse speeding, she groped blindly at the sheets on the bed. Where was he? She stumbled to the window, grabbed the sash and pulled. The sun streamed over an empty bed. Ida greeted her from the center of the kitchen, poised at attention with the rifle butt balanced on her foot, and the barrel pointed at the ceiling.

"Put that foolish gun away!" Celia ordered. "There are enough people dead already." She ran to catch up with Oscar.

The men had thrown off their coats and were brandishing rifles. Young Waldemar waved a group of them toward Siren's Cove and the Devil's Dance Floor.

She floundered through the rotting snow drifts behind Oscar, her soaked skirt clinging to her legs, and called after him. He waited impatiently, anxious to get back to the men. If Wagner still were foolish enough to be on any of the islands, the Shoalers would take justice into their own hands, Celia was certain of that. Oscar held out a hand to help her over a bank of snow. "I don't understand why the men weren't home. Where were Ivan Christensen, and John and Matthew Hontvet?" she thought out loud.

"Old Ingebretsen told me they went to Portsmouth for bait," Oscar said, shifting the rifle to his other shoulder. "They were going to return last night, but the bait must have come in on an early train this morning."

In sight of the Ingebretsen cottage, one of the children for whom Celia had always taken a fancy ran out to meet them, half crying and laughing. "Thora, dear," she said, drawing the child beneath a comforting arm and walking with her toward the cottage. She affectionately brushed the girl's tangled blond hair out of her eyes.

Oscar did an about face and disappeared over the hill.

The cottage wasn't as grand as the artists' bungalows nearer the hotel, but it was clean and trim. She entered the downstairs parlor. The blinds were still drawn, the flames had died out in the grate, and she wondered why Mrs. Ingebretsen should let the fire go out. At first she had trouble adjusting to the darkness after the glare of sunlight and snow. But then she saw Maren lying on a day bed beneath a mound of quilts and blankets.

Mrs. Ingebretsen came into the room. "Oh, Mrs. Thaxter, I so glad to see you," she said, embracing her. Like her husband, she possessed strong features, and her large build added to that strength.. She looked apologetically toward the grate. "I let fire go out. My husband tell me better accustom Maren to heat slowly."

Celia walked over to the swaddled woman, and nearly stepped on her little dog Ringe, who looked soulfully up at his mistress from the foot of the bed.

Maren was sobbing, her face tear-stained, her teeth chattering. She grasped Celia's hand and gripped it as if she were drowning and Celia was the only one who could save her. Celia felt the rough skin on her small hand and turned it over. The skin of the palm was scratched and torn in several places. In the dim light she barely could make out Maren's frightened face, but it too was scratched and she had a long ugly gash on her cheek.

Mrs. Ingebretsen unwrapped the towels, revealing Maren's bruised and swollen legs. "I don't know what to do, Mrs. Thaxter. I try to help the feet. You see? They so frozen, they not even bleed. We soak in warm water. Hands too. Now we try get going the blood with warm cloths. You think so?"

Celia still was recovering from the shock of seeing Maren so pale and beaten up. "Yes," she said, "you did the very right thing, Mrs. Ingebretsen."

The woman smiled, the first smile Celia had seen all day, and she felt considerably bolstered by it.

Again, Maren grabbed her hand and wouldn't let go. Her eyes burned with feverish urgency. "I tell you, Mrs. Thaxter. I tell you!"

"You should rest, Maren. Won't you sleep? I promise I'll sit right here beside you."

"I never sleep no more." Tears welled up in her eyes. "Please, Mrs. Thaxter. I tell you." She sat up all of a sudden and held Celia with surprising force in her small arms. Then pointing a trembling finger at the blood-stained gash on her cheek, she said, "See? Is where he hit me with chair." Furiously, Maren grappled at the towels around her feet while Celia tried to constrain her. "See my feet?"

Thora stood in the doorway with a tray of bread, jam, and tea, her thin adolescent body forlorn and unsure.

Celia struggled with the hysterical woman, persuading her to lie back under the covers. Then realizing that Thora should be kept busy, she asked her to fetch some arnica to bathe Maren's cuts and bruises.

Mrs. Ingebretsen smoothed back her greying hair. "Oh dear. We haven't," she said.

"My mother's bound to have some," Celia said, getting up.

"No. Please, Mrs. Thaxter. I tell you," Maren pleaded. Her trembling voice brought Celia nearly to tears herself. It was clear that Maren Hontvet would not be able to rest for a long while.

Celia sat back down on the side of the bed, and Maren, like someone obsessed with a terrible dark secret which they must tell or die, relived the nightmare she had experienced the night before.

"The men not come home," Maren whispered through chattering teeth. "My John, Anethe's Ivan, and John's brother go in the *Clara Bella* to Portsmouth. At supper we worry but Emil

Ingebretsen row to Smutty-Nose and say not to worry. They be back at midnight. It's first night we alone. But we have Ringe."

The little dog, hearing his name, looked up from the foot of the bed and cocked one ear.

Celia had no heart for this. Thora stood as if mesmerized at her mother's side.

"So we sit by fire and wait. Karen was going to Portsmouth look for work, but when Emil come she decides stay. So I make bed for Karen in kitchen, and Anethe and me sleeps in other room downstairs. We leave kitchen door open, and blinds too, because we like to see moon's light."

Celia listened intently, feeling at odds with her innate sense of curiosity and her love of a story.

"I'm asleep but Ringe he barks. I think the men come home. Karen call from kitchen, 'John is that you?' I not awake. Then I hear bangs like someone falling and breaking dishes. My John is never drunk so I jump up and run to door. But it's locked!"

Maren's eyes grew larger, her voice rose in panic. When Celia held her hand, Maren's fingernails dug into her skin. "Are you sure you want to tell us now?" she asked.

"Please. I tell you, Mrs. Thaxter." Her teeth no longer chattered, and two spots of red had appeared in her deathly white face.

"I shake door and try get out. Karen screams, 'John kills me! John kills me!' My John kill my sister? It's not right. Something fall on door and crash it open. I see Karen on floor. I see tall man in moon's light on other side of kitchen. I so afraid. Is not my John. I call 'Anethe! Go out window. Run! Hide!' Man is pushing door. Karen not help me. She is hurting on floor. I tell Anethe scream. But she too afraid. I think someone hear us scream. I want scream but too tired. I can't shut door no longer."

"Oh, my God," Celia whispered.

Maren rushed on in a frenzy. "Then man stop push door. Anethe crawl out window. She say me she cannot move. So I go help. Anethe stand in nightdress in moon's light and she cry 'Louis! Louis!'"

The color returned to Maren's cheeks, and her voice reached a high excited pitch. But Celia could tell she was wearing out because the grip on her hand relaxed.

"Man have axe. I leave axe near well for to break the ice. I see him hit Anethe with it. I goes crazy. I look for Karen so we hide. But Karen say, 'I cannot! I cannot!' I try to lift her but she don't move. I pick up Ringe."

The dog uncurled and suddenly barked. Celia picked him up, petted him, and placed him in Maren's arms. She buried her face in his fur. The sobs came uncontrollably, but Maren went on. "I throw skirt over me. No time shoes. Nothing. I think where I can hide. Man light lamp and look for me. First I think to take man's boat. But I'm not finding it. So I run to empty house near water. I so afraid my dog barks. I hear Karen scream and I know man is killing Karen.

"I not know time but moon is going and I run in snow to end of Smutty-Nose. I so close to being in water I feel it on my feet. I crawl in rocks so if man follow he don't see me.

"I don't move. I not breathe. I hear feet so close I see pants legs. I keep my hand on Ringe's mouth." Maren hugged the dog so tightly it yelped.

"Three times man come so near I hear breathe. I so frighten I think I am dead. When sun come I cannot move. I am froze. I rub feet with sand. My feet stick to rocks. I hear working men on Star Island, and when I wave my skirt they stop, but they don't come."

Celia listened. Yes, she did remember the workmen had stopped hammering a few minutes that morning.

"So I walks to other end where house is. I think in day's light man not be there. I want to go in house. But I cannot look."

Maren broke down again, and Celia cradled her in her arms, urging her to stop and tell them later. But Maren shook her head.

Celia brushed the tears from her own eyes, and Thora ran out of the room.

"Blinds in my house is down. We leave them open when we goes to bed." Maren's broken voice turned hard as steel. "Man is hiding his filthy murder! I run to sea wall and I stand on it. I wave at children until throat hurts. Children get father and he comes for me in boat —."

Maren's voice trailed off as she slumped back onto the pillows. But her troubled eyes remained wide open, and she would not let go of Celia's hand.

16

As Maren stared vacantly at the ceiling, Celia's mind kept returning to Betty Moody who had escaped near-death by hiding on Star Island. When the woman saw an Indian scouting party canoeing toward the shoals, she scrambled into a cave with her baby in her arms. But the infant started crying and the distressed mother clapped a hand over its mouth to smother the cries. After the natives rowed away, Betty crept out of the cave, rejoicing that she and her baby had been spared, only to discover she'd smothered her child to death.

Celia always told this tale to titillate idle summer guests. But now, Betty Moody's fear and anxiety seemed all too real, and the sense of safety and well-being Celia always felt when she was on Appledore had been violated.

As she made her way to her mother's, Celia spotted sails beating a favorable wind, and with dread, realized it must be the men on the *Clara Bella*. They would be tired after their night in Portsmouth and looking forward to a good hearty breakfast. She turned around, and sludged through the melting snow back toward Ingebretsen's cottage to meet them when they arrived.

Fortunately, some of the men from the hunting party had seen the *Clara Bella* and were waving it toward Appledore so that the Norwegians wouldn't sail straight toward the scene of horror on Smutty-Nose. Anethe and Ivan had just been married and were so very much in love. He would be inconsolable.

Celia and Mrs. Ingebretsen stood on the granite lintel watching the men climb from the beach. Ivan ran up the path first.

Carpenter Ingebretsen staggered behind. "I tried to tell him," he said, throwing his huge hands into the air in a helpless gesture. "But he don't listen."

Celia prepared herself to tell Ivan if nobody else did, but before she could speak he rushed into the darkened parlor and found Maren. "Where's Anethe!" he shouted, his face taut and full of worry.

Maren looked past her excited brother and toward her husband John who stood behind him in the doorway. Tears trickled down her bruised cheek. John Hontvet pushed past Ivan, and placed his rough hand tenderly on her brow.

Looking wildly about the room Ivan repeated, "Where's Anethe?"

Maren held onto John, rocking back and forth in his arms. Apprehensively, she looked over her husband's shoulder and toward her brother Ivan. John held his wife arm's length, looking into her eyes with direct firmness. "Are you all right?" he asked. She nodded. "Then you must tell Ivan," he said.

Maren looked into her husband's face, and then past him at Ivan. "She's—. She's—."

Her brother fell to his knees by the bed. "Tell me Anethe's all right."

Tears streamed down Maren's face. Before any of them could say a word, Ivan jumped to his feet and dashed out the door.

John touched his wife's head with one large hand and turned it toward him. "I be back and you tell everything." He kissed her gently, then raced after Ivan.

Mrs. Ingebretsen, Celia, and Maren formed a silent triangle in the dark empty room. The door ajar, they heard the dory as it scraped the sand when the men shoved off.

Maren buried her face in her hands. "Oh, God. I could not say Anethe dead. I could not."

Celia held Maren's shaking body. She imagined the men pulling up their boats and climbing the incline to the Hontvet house on Smutty-Nose. They would find Anethe first, sprawled in her nightgown on the ground, her long blond hair caked with blood.

Celia tried to dismiss the tantalizing odors of corned beef and cabbage emanating from her mother's cottage as the servants crowded around her in the kitchen. "Did you see the bodies, Mrs. Thaxter?" Ida asked, gawking as Celia fell into a chair and took off her boots.

"Of course not!" she answered sharply, looking at them huddled and waiting like vultures for the sordid details. Knowing that she would not get away with silence, as briefly as possible she recounted Maren's tale. Better to lay out the truth than have them read it distorted in tomorrow's newspapers.

Ida sashayed forward. "I bet Wagner had his way with 'em first. I hear he was a ladies man if ever there was one."

That did it. Celia stood up, hands on her hips, and immediately they stopped their clammering to listen. "I want it understood.

Not one of you—not one—do you hear, is to set foot on Smutty-Nose until the police have arrived and the investigation is over."

"But—." Ida blurted out.

She closed her arms over her chest. "It will not do to have you snooping around and spreading rumors. Nor are you to visit Maren and John unless they ask for you. Is that clear?"

They nodded agreement, except Ida who scowled. "And after the investigation?" she muttered under her breath.

"That is up to you, my dear." All at once Celia felt tired and defenseless. "I prefer remembering Karen and Anethe as they were, not smeared with insinuations such as I've heard in this kitchen." She turned so that none of them could see the tears at the corners of her eyes.

The Laightons cloistered around the dining table, each bowed in reflective silence. Karl's place was empty.

"I'll call him, mum," the maid said. "I think he's in his workroom." She ambled off to fetch him.

Oscar whistled a long low exclamation. "That girl is slower than syrup in January."

Cedric had eaten little, staring gloomily at his plate. No wonder, Celia thought. He'd been to Smutty-Nose with the other men and seen the mayhem. "I'm taking John Hontvet to the police station in Portsmouth this afternoon," he told them.

Karl charged into the room, his hair disheveled, hands stained with chemicals. Celia kissed his unshaven cheek. All of her sons were thin and rather fragile looking. Much as she hated to admit it, they took after Levi.

"What have you been up to all morning, little spud?" she asked. "I'm afraid Mother has been neglecting you." Karl stabbed his fork into a whole boiled potato and held it up to eat it. "Remember your manners!"

Obediently, he put down the potato and removed the skin, cross-hatching it to pieces with a knife. Sometimes Celia wondered if she should let him work alone with photographic chemicals. But Oscar and Cedric had spent weeks instructing him and assured her he knew what he was doing.

"What were you up to this morning? You were up awfully early," she told him.

"Can I show you, Mama?" Karl wiped his mouth and started from the table but sat back down. Any other time he'd pester her until she gave in, but today his eyes were shiny and he focused them on something far away. Just as well. Celia was beginning to feel the strain of the morning.

After supper Cedric left for Portsmouth, and she let Karl lead her back to the chilly darkroom.

The previous summer they had built a twenty-foot high, six-sided building which piped gas to the hotel and adjacent cottages. Unfortunately, her brothers hadn't gotten around to putting up the proper fixtures in Karl's workshop.

As they entered the dingy room, she became aware of the odors of oil, sawdust and chemicals, and decided she liked them. Why was it men had such a natural propensity for how things worked? Oscar was good at fixing things and had applied for some patents. And Karl, who could barely read, loved to tinker with broken gadgets. Several people at the hotel had commented favorably about the quality of his photographs, too.

"Look, Mama." Karl held a print of the Laighton cottage to the light.

"Who's that?" she asked, pointing out a figure half hidden by a curtain.

Karl picked up a magnifying glass and held it to the print. "Gee, I didn't see her before, Mama. It's Karen."

Oscar, who had been puttering in a corner, walked over and looked at the print. The picture of Karen sent a wave of uneasiness through Celia.

Karl's voice surged with high-pitched excitement. "Karen and I are going on a picnic!"

She signaled Oscar to change the subject.

"Karen promised to take me on a picnic!" Karl stamped his good leg and waved the photo in the air.

"Let me explain," Celia said, groping for the words to tell Karl his friends were dead.

His eyes flashed, and he took the photograph by each corner and ripped it in two. "She lied to me. She's gone for good." He snatched another snapshot from Oscar and ripped that too.

"Listen to me, Karl," Celia pleaded.

Oscar grabbed his flailing arms and held them fast. "You've got to tell him, Celia," Oscar said between clenched teeth, restraining Karl, who had gone haywire. Then, Karl went limp and sullen as usual after one of his fits. "She might as well be dead," he said, biting a trembling lip.

She and Oscar faced each other in total surprise. Karl's statement, she was sure, had been said without the least knowledge of its implications. Her son had hurled it at them like a child that says he wishes he were dead without really knowing the meaning of death.

Karl went to his bedroom without a fuss, and when he was lying down she asked, "Now why did you rip up that fine print? Mother wanted to look at it again."

He blinked at her with innocent concern. "I'll make another one, Mama."

She turned away an instant. How did you tell a child of twenty-one that his best friends had been murdered? "Karl—" she began.

"Yes, Mama."

"Karen and Anethe are dead."

His expression told her he didn't understand.

"Remember when you and Mother found a sea gull washed onto the beach. Anethe and Karen have gone like the sea gull, and they're with God now."

She had thought that telling Karl would bring her a feeling of release, but as she looked at his puzzled face, she realized he still didn't understand.

The grandfather clock in the vestibule had just struck ten when they heard voices down by the landing wharf. She went to the door and watched the officers filing toward the Ingebretsen's, holding lanterns high as they snaked over the jagged, unfamiliar rocks.

Cedric raced uphill toward his sister. "They'll be over here as soon as they get through questioning Maren." He shrugged. "I guess it's just a formality. Maren made it pretty clear that Louis Wagner did it. In fact, they've already sent the Portsmouth marshall to Boston to look for him."

Oscar put down his hand of cards. Karl pouted. "Come on, Uncle Oscar. We're not finished playing."

"It's time for bed, Karl." Celia motioned for him to leave.

"Tell you what, Karly," Oscar said. "I'll keep my hand just the way it is and we'll finish tomorrow."

When Karl was safely out of earshot, Cedric continued. "What an awful day. I had to go and see the whole bloody mess with the coroner's men. It looks like robbery. How much actually was stolen isn't certain, but John Hontvet said the hundred and thirty-five dollars he had hidden at the bottom of the mattress was still there. Maren thinks that Wagner took twenty dollars cash from a kitchen drawer."

Eliza Laighton shook her head sadly. "The lives of two lovely women for twenty dollars."

Someone knocked on the cottage door. Ordinarily they left it unbolted. Celia slid back the iron bar to let in Carpenter Ingebretsen, a blue-coated officer, and half a dozen men, one of which she recognized as a reporter.

"I'm Deputy Sheriff Philbrick," the officer said, stepping forward. "Sorry to disturb you at this late hour— but these men are on the coroner's jury." The sheriff shuffled uncomfortably in place. "This will take only a few minutes. We just want to make sure we haven't missed anything."

Cedric introduced his mother, brother, and sister. Meanwhile, Oscar had assembled the servants. They clustered near the doorway in a peculiarly ragtag group. Ida was in her nightdress. Several men had dressed in a hurry and their nightshirts trailed from the waists of their work pants. The summer staff hadn't been hired yet, so at most there were a dozen of them.

"I'm sure you're all aware of what happened last night on Smutty-Nose," the sheriff said. A few of them responded, a few nodded, and one yawned. "I'm sorry to call you from your sleep like this, but this is a serious matter."

"Oh, yes, Sir," Ida chimed in. Then, aware that Sheriff Philbrick was staring at her, she discovered the top of her nightdress opened and quickly fumbled to button it up.

"The reason I've summoned you is to find out if any of you happened to see a row boat last night, or saw a suspicious looking man either on Smutty-Nose or Appledore Island?"

One of the old-timers shuffled forward in a worn pair of slippers, dragging a wool blanket along the floor. "Well, Sir," he said, stroking his beard stained with tobacco juice. "I was sound asleep. Wan't I, E'l?"

Earl smiled. "How should I know, Ben, I was sawin' logs m'sef."

The sheriff started to smile but kept a poker face. "Has any of you seen Louis Wagner around here these past few days?"

Celia looked from one to another. They were a motley lot, but good-hearted. Most of them hadn't two pennies to rub together, and she and her mother had taken them in and trained them for service. Once in awhile one of her family would find a maid's closet filled with stolen linens, but that was rare. "If any of them saw anything unusual," she told the sheriff, "I'm sure they would say so. I've already asked them not to go to Smutty-Nose until the investigation is over."

"Quite right," the sheriff said. "Well, then, thank you for your patience. You may all go back to bed." After the last of the group plodded out, Eliza Laighton offered the men something to drink. "That 's kind of you, Mrs. Laighton, and I'm sure the men would enjoy some comfort after what they've seen this afternoon. However, there are just a few questions I'd like to ask your family first, if you don't object?"

Celia eyed the reporter busily scribbling away. What could he possibly find to write? Nothing of any significance had been said so far.

The sheriff quickly but methodically looked around the room. "Are all present who were here last night from midnight until approximately seven o'clock this morning?"

Her mother nodded. Celia nodded. Oscar nodded. Cedric blinked and started to speak.

"Yes, Mr. Laighton?" the sheriff asked, leaning forward.

"I was just going to say it was the first calm night we've had in two weeks. We all went to bed thinking spring had arrived."

"Quite right." The sheriff sighed. He looked tired. "I usually don't pay much attention to weather, but I'm sadly aware the sea was smooth as glass last night."

The coroner's men stood back and let the reporter step forward. "I'd like to ask Mrs. Thaxter a few questions."

The sheriff's pleasant demeanor changed noticeably. Standing straighter, he told the reporter, "This is an investigation, not an interview."

Undaunted, the reporter stood his ground. "Mrs. Thaxter's father worked on a newspaper and I'm sure she's aware of how important accuracy is in a case of homicide."

The man was short. He wore a bowler and bright checkered coat, and his eyes shifted here and there as though he were missing nothing. He reminded Celia of a small insistent weasel.

Sheriff Philbrick, on the other hand, was tall. His stature alone commanded attention. He squelched the reporter simply by stepping in front of him, then turned to Eliza Laighton. "And now, we'd be grateful for something hot to drink before the long ride back to Portsmouth. I doubt we'll reach the mainland before three in the morning."

Cedric and Oscar pulled up some more chairs while Celia followed her mother into the kitchen. She was waylaid by the persistent reporter. "Mrs. Thaxter, just a word."

"You heard Sheriff Philbrick."

"Sure, sure," he said and smiled, "but there's no harm asking, is there?"

She tried to edge sideways through the door but realized there wasn't room for both of them, and dreaded touching the nosey little man.

"Where's your husband, Mrs. Thaxter?"

Why wouldn't the bothersome man leave her alone? Hadn't she been through enough already? When she didn't answer his first question, he followed with a second. "I understand you have three sons. Where are they?"

Sheriff Philbrick came up behind the reporter and accosted him in a booming voice. "Mrs. Thaxter's personal life is none of your damned business," he said. "And if I find you making a nuisance of yourself once more, I'll have your editor pull you off this story."

While they were at each other's throats, down the hall Celia saw Karl cross from the water closet to his bedroom. She closed her eyes and brought her hand to her mouth, dizzy with sudden dread. "Now look what you've done," the sheriff hissed at the reporter. "For God's sake, get out!"

17

Here was a lesson to be learned —you certainly could not believe everything you read in the newspapers. Celia picked up two accounts of the murders and compared them. Both said that Louis Wagner had been seen at Tucker's Wharf with an axe in his hand. But *The Daily Chronicle* referred to Maren's testimony that the axe was "by the door." *The Evening Times*, on the other hand, wrote that Wagner "killed the two young women with the axe," implying that Wagner had carried the axe with him in the boat all the way from Tucker's Wharf. This would mean premeditated murder, and Celia distinctly remembered Maren telling her that the man had taken the axe she used to chop ice off the well.

But what particularly disturbed her were the distortions of the facts relating to the arrest of Wagner. The account was explicit enough. Marshall Johnson had gone to Boston where he called on the police chief. After some detective work based on photographs of Wagner which Johnson had with him, Wagner was taken into custody and sent back on a train to Portsmouth. Crowds gathered along the tracks and at the stations. Bricks were thrown and pistols brandished at the alleged murderer.

This is where factual information left off and subjective commentary began. *The Daily Chronical* wrote: "We should not select Wagner in a crowd as one who would commit murder, as his expression is one of kindness."

Celia remembered Louis Wagner from the Sunday she had met him, and "kindness" was far from the word she'd use to describe him. But that wasn't the point. The point was that the journalist had injected a personal bias that didn't belong in newspaper writing. *The Evening Times* also was at fault. It blithely pitted Maren's testimony against Wagner's good looks and persuasive charms and made Maren seem the fool.

Celia reread the newspaper account and wondered if this possibly could be the same Louis Wagner she had met at the chapel on Star Island.

> He looks everybody squarely in the face, talks frankly and freely with a slight foreign accent, and in all respects acts and talks like an honest, intelligent man.

She ran her finger down the newspaper column until she came to the part about Maren, and her anger mounted. How could they speculate this way before the trial? It was so unfair to Maren who tried to remember every detail, although the constant questioning was destroying her.

> In spite of the strong circumstantial evidence against Louis Wagner, it must be admitted that there is room for a reasonable doubt as to his guilt. Maren Hontvet did not see the face of the murderer. She only saw him as she looked out the window, and then his back was turned toward her.

Not once did they mention that the moonlight would have enhanced Maren's identification of the man, or that she was familiar enough with Wagner since he had stayed with them awhile.

She shoved the paper out of sight when Karl came into the room. "What are those people doing?" he asked, pointing out the window at boats heading for the beach at Smutty-Nose. "Are they going to see Anethe and Karen?"

"Karl, don't you remember? I told you. Karen and Anethe are dead."

"Karen and Anethe are dead, Mama?"

"Yes, Karly." The poor boy. He truly didn't fathom the simplest things.

"And that's why the *Mayflower* is bringing all those people out here?"

"Yes, dear."

He asked no more questions, but something was gnawing away at her that she couldn't explain, and the longer it took to prove Wagner's guilt, the worse it became. She remembered a similar feeling years ago when she was a child. She and her brothers had been playing one rainy day and one of them knocked over her mother's favorite lamp. Cedric and Oscar dashed out of the room so they wouldn't be caught, but she couldn't move.

"Who did this, Celia?" her mother asked, stooping to collect the pieces of the prized lamp. It had been a favorite of hers, too, and now the dusky roses painted on the large round globe were shattered at her feet. "I did," she lied, blinking back her tears. Afterward, when she was sent to her room without dinner, she wondered why she had confessed to an act that she hadn't committed. In her heart she knew that she hadn't done it to protect her brothers. The truth was that although she hadn't broken the lamp she still felt terribly guilty.

And that was how she felt now with Anethe and Karen dead, Karl sulking around the house, and Louis Wagner running loose. The feeling might have gone away if she hadn't overheard Ida whispering to Ben, "The murderer could be a workman on Star Island, or for that matter, any one of us on Appledore."

If Wagner weren't found guilty, would the sheriff return for a thorough investigation, and would he question Karl? Only the other evening she had been sitting on the *chaise longue* in her bedroom reading a book when she discovered Karl's little diary pushed beneath one of the silk cushions. She opened it to the title page. *Pocket Diary, l873.* The only other printing was Karl's name in big awkward letters. At the back was a small accordion pocket. She squeezed it open and a piece of paper fell out: "Do not fight or scold or be sassy or be notty and be good at the table and don't taulk as much as you can help."

Celia smiled, and carefully replaced Karl's pledge, hiding it where she'd found it.

Did her responsibilities as mother and guardian to her slow-witted son give her the right to read his personal diary? What could she hope to find? That he couldn't spell? That he could barely write? That he was given to exaggerated statements? But, she rationalized, how was she to help him if she didn't know what he was thinking?

She took up the diary again and turned to March. The first, second, and third pages were blank. Under March 4 was Karl's clumsy attempt at an entry. "Can't go outside. Mother won't let me see Anethe and Karen. I hate Anethe. I hate Karen. Sometimes I wish —."

The last part had been erased. She should have expected as much. His anger had to give vent during that interminable snowstorm. Then it occurred to her that he'd written his childish secrets two days prior to the killings. And suddenly she felt alarmed. What if Wagner weren't convicted? What if the diary were to end up in the hands of the sheriff? Couldn't it be used as circumstantial evidence against her son?

The diary must be destroyed.

With quick and clear determination, she lighted the stove and fed the fire with diary pages until flames shot up the stovepipe, curled, blackened, and settled to ashes in the grate. If Karl were to ask for the diary, she would tell him she hadn't seen it and promise to buy him another.

Celia spread the morning newspaper on her desk, scanning it for news concerning the inquiry and came across a neatly boxed advertisement.

> THE ISLES OF SHOALS MURDER
> For 25 cents I will send an excellent photograph of Wagner, the ISLES OF SHOALS MURDERER, taken by Webber while at the police station in Saco.

She shook her head in disgust. It was going to be what Cedric called "a wild summer" with tourists clambering over Smutty-Nose looking for souvenirs. Of course, it would mean good business for the hotel, but the thought of them filing past Maren's cottage filled her with dismay.

Wagner's arraignment was announced a week after the murders, and testimony given in South Berwick, Maine, since Smutty-Nose was in Maine's jurisdiction. Celia ruled out any notion of going. She wanted to keep her name out of the newspapers, and as it happened, she made a wise decision because everyone from miles around went to hear the testimony. She surely would have been recognized.

While she was busy worrying about Karl, her brothers were worrying that they might be called forward. But there was no motive. After all, they owned the hotel and were financially self sufficient. Karl, on the other hand, had never earned a penny and received a nominal allowance. Not to mention the fact that the mentally deficient were widely believed to be violent and uncontrollable. Celia was sure that she'd never be able to make Sheriff Philbrick understand how harmless Karl really was.

By the final week of the trial in Alfred, Maine, she desperately wanted to be there to hear the witnesses and see Louis Wagner on the stand. He had to be guilty, and yet Ida's words kept coming back to her: "The murderer could be a workman on Star Island, or for that matter, any one of us on Appledore."

She put on her darkest, most inconspicuous dress and bought passage with an enterprising fisherman taking a boatload of Shoalers to the mainland so they could attend the trial. In Portsmouth she soon discovered that every pleasure wagon, stage, and hack had been hired to and from the Alfred courthouse. The train was no exception; the car was jammed with excited passengers who had closely followed the inquest. Celia pretended to read a newspaper as she eavesdropped, surprised at her piqued curiosity.

"My uncle is David Burke, you know, the man Wagner stole the boat from to get to the Shoals," one lad bragged.

"Is that so? Do you think that will get us in?" someone wisecracked.

"Did you read about the other murder Wagner committed?" a plump matron asked the gentleman across from her.

"Why, no! Tell me about it."

"Well, it seems that Wagner was a seaman at the time. He persuaded a buddy of his to take his bank book with him on the ship instead of leaving it with the landlady as he usually did."

"And —."

"And the buddy was reported to have fallen overboard." Here the matron raised her voice but lowered her head so that it formed a shield between her and the other passengers. "Next day Wagner presented his drowned buddy's bank book to the bank teller."

"You don't say!"

18

It had been foolish of Celia to fear recognition from such a mob. She was just another body bobbing through the unruly, curious spectators. Once safely inside the spacious courtroom, she discovered a bench against the back wall and squeezed through the milling crowd into a vacant seat. She was lucky to have spotted it, because people were blocking the aisles and had been ordered to move outside. With a raised arm a troublemaker yelled, "Let Wagner swing!" When a bystander took a jab at his right ear, officers closed in and hauled both of them from the room.

Finally, when the aisles had been cleared, a cordon of policemen guarded the back doors while the crowd outside jeered, angered that they'd been excluded from the trial of the century. Most of the women were accompanied by their husbands, and Celia regretted she'd brought no one along. The excited throng beating against the back doors frightened her.

Judge Barrows took his place on the bench and slammed his gavel on the rostrum. "Order in the court!" he shouted. "Before this trial begins, I must warn you that heckling and disorderly conduct will not be tolerated."

The State prosecutors filed to tables at the front of the courtroom to the stomping of feet and a loud cheer. Despite the judge's warning, Louis Wagner and his lawyer were greeted by boos and hissing. He was thinner and paler than when Celia had seen him on that memorable Sunday last summer. She caught a hint of the braggadocio in his eyes as he surveyed the audience, but this quickly was followed by a look of contrition and humility.

"Lynch the bastard!" a man shouted, bolting from his seat with a clinched fist. Immediately, two policemen locked each of his arms and swung him between them down the aisle. As the back door opened to let them pass, they could hear the hooting crowd outside.

"This court is now in session," Judge Barrows declared. "I call on the prosecuting attorney for the State of Maine."

Attorney General Plaisted rose and addressed the judge:

"At the Judicial Court of Alfred, Maine, within York County on the seventeeth of June in the year of our Lord one thousand eight hundred and seventy-three, the State presents that Louis H. Wagner of Portsmouth in the County of Rockingham and State of New Hampshire on the sixth day of March last at an island called Smutty-Nose, did feloniously, willfully, and of malice aforethought, kill and murder Karen Christensen and Anethe Hontvet, against the peace of the State and contrary to statute."

Wagner's lawyer stood. "Your Honor, at this time the respondent moves that the indictment be suspended."

A chorus of ohs and ahs arose from the spectators, and the judge raised a hand for silence. "Please proceed," he ordered.

Wagner's lawyer continued. "The place where the alleged offense was committed is indefinite and uncertain, and not in conformity with the law."

Celia wondered what he was driving at. Ask anyone from the Shoals and they'd tell you. Smutty-Nose was in Maine. Was this a trick for a mistrial?

A dark furrow divided the judge's brow. "It is agreed that if any question pertaining to jurisdiction arises in this case, it will be considered at that time. Otherwise, we must proceed."

Maren was the first witness called by the State. Assisted by an officer, she limped into the courtroom. The frail woman raised her hand and in a shaky, halting voice promised to tell the truth and nothing but the truth. As Celia listened, she realized that Maren's urgency to relive that fateful night had been supplanted by a tone of resignation. The brave Norwegian woman had survived by sheer will and wit, only to become a victim of hounding lawyers.

The District Attorney cleared his throat. "While Louis Wagner boarded with you, Mrs. Hontvet, was Karen Christensen also living with you on Smutty-Nose?"

"Sometimes."

"And did she sleep under the same roof when Wagner was a boarder at your cottage?"

"No, Sir."

"Do you know if Karen owned a piece of silver?"

"Yes, Sir. She got from someone at hotel on Hog."

The lawyer looked confused.

"We sometimes say Appledore Island is Hog, Sir," Maren explained.

"And on March fifth did you see Karen's piece of silver?"

"Yes. I ask Karen to buy button and I give her button like it.

When I put white button in coin purse, I see Karen's silver. Men is not coming home so she don't go after all. She stay with us."

The prosecutor smiled at Maren. "Thank you, you may step down." Surprised that it was over already, she remained seated until the officer took her arm, and she recovered her seat at the side while the officer escorted her husband to the stand.

John Hontvet described how he had found Anethe with a crushed bone above one eye, and both ears severed. A chair had been broken, and the smashed clock had stopped at seven past one. In the other room he'd found Karen with a fractured skull, and blood smeared on the bed sheets where their nest egg had been stashed and miraculously undiscovered.

Celia took a deep breath when John told the lawyer how easy it was for a man to row to the Shoals on a calm night and that he had done it many times. Fortunately, there had been witnesses on the mainland who had seen John in Portsmouth the night of the murders.

Elizabeth Johnson next took the stand. She was known to Celia by name only; the Norwegians often stayed at her boarding house when they went to Portsmouth. She was a soft-spoken woman and spectators craned in their seats to catch snatches of her testimony:

"I live at Webster Street. My husband Matthew is invalid. In March Louis Wagner stay at my house. Night March five Wagner is not sleeping there so I fasten back door at midnight. I am first one awake and see Wagner about seven-thirty coming by back gate. I say, 'Well, Louis, where you come from?' I say to him John Hontvet baits trawls and not see him. Then Louis tell my husband he feel bad and my husband say for him to take some medicines. But Louis say he not really sick. He just feel bad because of some troubles."

Mr. Tapley, Wagner's Boston lawyer, asked Mrs. Johnson to remain on the stand, and not only did he keep her there, but went at her like the Grand Inquisitor. Celia shuddered to think how she herself would withstand a similar barrage of insinuations and insults.

"What time did you fasten the door, Mrs. Johnson?"

"Midnight."

"And just how did you know it was midnight?"

"My husband is invalid. He waiting see if Wagner come. My daughter she is sewing. When I find John and Ivan is baiting trawls I think Wagner gone, so I say husband I am locking door."

Tapley drummed his fingers on the table. "All right, Mrs. Johnson. You needn't elaborate. You still haven't explained how you knew it was midnight."

"I know it is not one o'clock."

"Oh, I see. That's good. Since it wasn't one o'clock, it must have been midnight." The defense lawyer put both hands in his pockets and, smiling, walked toward the jury box.

Elizabeth Johnson blushed. "I know it by our clock."

"And what kind of clock is it?"

"A good clock. I have it twenty years and it work fine," she said indignantly.

Someone in the back of the courtroom laughed.

"And when did you look at this fine clock?"

"I think about midnight," she said, her voice faltering.

"Not precisely midnight?"

"It was after midnight when I fasten door."

"And when did you unfasten the door?"

"It might be six o'clock, or between five and six."

The judge interrupted. "Mr. Tapley, let us get on with your line of questioning, shall we?"

Mrs. Johnson nervously tucked a curl under her bonnet.

"Would you say Wagner was a man of peaceable habits?" Tapley prodded.

"He treat me nice. He never say bad words."

The State Prosecutor stood. "Your Honor, I request that Mrs. Johnson's last answer be stricken from the record. Mr. Tapley is putting words into the woman's mouth."

"I agree, Mr. Plaisted. Clerk, strike Mr. Tapley's last question. You may resume."

The defense lawyer addressed the judge. "Your Honor, I have nothing further at this time."

Mrs. Johnson's daughter followed as a witness for the State, and what the mother lacked in spunk, Mary Johnson more than made up for. She was about twenty years old, not beautiful but fetching in a pert sort of way. Yes, she had known Louis Wagner. He shared rooms at the head of the stairs with Fred Moore and William Kenniston. Yes, she saw him go out at about eight o'clock on the morning of March sixth. He'd told her he was in some kind of trouble, and she had noticed blisters on his knuckles.

"And what was Wagner wearing. Do you know?"

"Yes. He had on a plain white shirt."

"How is it that you are able to identify it?"

"Well, underneath, the collar was torn and the buttonhole enlarged. I sewed it for him the afternoon of March fifth because it was the only shirt he had."

"And when did you next see this shirt?"

"The Monday after the murders, Sir, when you took it from the vault and showed it to me."

Plaisted held up a soiled white shirt.

"Yes, Sir. There is the buttonhole I sewed."

The Prosecutor picked up a manila envelope and dropped something from it into Mary Johnson's outstretched hand. The young girl examined the objects closely before Attorney Plaisted put it back into the envelope. "Mary, you've looked over four buttons. Do you recognize any of them as belonging to the clothes of Louis Wagner?"

"No, Sir."

"And do you know every button you sew onto the boarders' shirts?"

The girl hesitated. "No, Sir, but Wagner only had one shirt and no buttons were missing. I checked when I mended the buttonhole. Only the buttonhole was enlarged."

"Thank you, Miss Johnson. You've been extremely helpful. The defense may cross-examine."

Tapley walked up to the girl. "What time in the morning did you talk with Louis Wagner?"

"Between nine and ten o'clock."

"A few moments ago you said you talked with him at eight."

"Oh, no, Mr. Tapley. I said I saw Mr. Wagner between eight and nine o'clock, but I talked with him between nine and ten o'clock."

The girl had caught the lawyer in his own game and he wasn't happy about it. "Do go on," he said in a vexed tone.

"I watched him because he acted queer."

"Did you mention this to your mother?"

"Not only to Mother, but to Father, and later to policeman Entwistle as well. It was about nine when I talked to him. I remember because my sister didn't leave for school until eight-thirty and that morning she was late."

Seeing that he was getting nowhere and might even be injuring his case, Tapley dismissed the girl.

The next witness called by the prosecution caused quite a stir as she took the stand. She wore garish ribbons and bows and her cheeks glowed with rouge.

Plaisted walked up to her and leaned nonchalantly on the rail of the witness box. "Miss Miller, tell us your occupation."

"Can't ya see that?" someone from the back shouted to outbursts of laughter.

The judge rapped his gavel. "One more outburst and you will be barred from this courtroom." He nodded at Plaisted to resume.

"I was working for Mrs. Brown in Boston. She ran a boarding house for sailors."

"Is that what ya call it?" someone else yelled. They all looked around but couldn't pick out the culprit.

"I first known Louis as Louis Ludwick."

Wagner suddenly stood and faced the judge. "That's not me, Your Honor," he protested, his back to the courtroom.

The judge placed both hands on the edges of the bench and leaned forward. "Mr. Wagner, you will have your turn to speak. I must ask that you remain silent until then. The counsel for the State may continue."

"And where did you see Louis Wagner, or Louis Ludwick as you call him?"

"At Mrs. Brown's on March sixth. I said, 'Good afternoon, Louis,' and he said I must be mistaken. I told him I wasn't and he admitted it was him. I told him he looked frightful and I asked him what had happened. He said he'd just murdered two sailors, and the mate had put him ashore. He'd shaved his beard so he wouldn't be recognized. He also said there was a woman he wanted to kill because he'd bought her fancy clothes and she'd run off to New York."

Plaisted paused, eyeing the jury and giving them time for this sensational new testimony to sink in. "Mr. Wagner actually said he murdered two sailors and wanted to kill a woman?"

She tossed her head and arched one eyebrow. "Would I lie, Your Honor?"

Aware of what kind of witness he was dealing with, Plaisted quickly changed the subject. "Do you remember having been on the Isles of Shoals three years ago, Miss Miller?"

"Sure. I went to Smutty-Nose for four months and was charged for disorderly conduct because my brother wanted me to leave and I didn't want to. You see, the prize fights was being held on Smutty-Nose and I wanted to see 'em. They was called off."

"And was Louis Wagner, or Louis Ludwick as you call him, there?"

"I don't rightly remember, Sir."

"I see. So in Boston you worked for Mrs. Brown. Is that it?"

"Yes, Sir."

"And what was the character of that house?"

"It was of lousy character."

A crescendo of whispers and laughter swept across the courtroom.

"That will be all, Your Honor. I have no further questions."

Miss Miller stepped down to a few cat calls, and the Prosecutor called the police sergeant who had been at the station when Wagner was searched.

"Sergeant, please tell the court what took place after Louis Wagner was apprehended."

"Well, Sir, we took him into a private room and I asked him if he had a boat. He told me it was on Smutty-Nose. I asked him if it was in anyone's charge and he said no. I told him that seemed strange. And he said he intended to go back and get it. I asked if he had supper at the Johnson's the previous evening and he said he had. He had on two shirts, a plaid one over an undershirt. We took them off to search him. He also had a silver piece, some coppers, a plug of tobacco, two pair of pants, and a hat."

"Two pair of pants?"

"A plaid pair under a newer pair."

"And the hat?"

"I think that Marshall Johnson, who also was questioning, asked him what kind of hat he wore to the island, and wasn't it a tall one? And Wagner denied owning a tall hat."

"Then what did Louis Wagner have on his head when he was arrested?"

"Just a plain black hat."

"Did it look new, sergeant?"

"Why, yes, Sir, it did."

As the sergeant stepped down and the next witness was called, Celia tried to remember if Maren had said the man she saw that night was wearing a hat. Then she tried to remember what kind of hat Louis had been wearing to church that day. But all that came to mind was John Whittier stepping out of the boat.

After this, a series of minor witnesses took the stand. A fisherman testified that he'd never known anyone to blister his knuckles baiting trawls, but you could get blood blisters on the sides of your knuckles from pulling oars.

Policeman Entwistle said that Wagner had told him that fishhooks made the blisters. He also related how he had found the blood-stained white shirt stuffed into a corner of the Johnson privy.

Another man with a sharp memory claimed that while they both were boarding at Johnson's he'd seen Wagner use a red pencil with teeth marks on one end and whittled at the other. He swore that this pencil was the same one now on exhibit as evidence on the table at the front of the courtroom.

Ingebreten's son Emil was called by the State and cross-examined by Tapley. He was the one who had found the red pencil and given it to one of the officers. Tapley walked up to the boy. "Exactly how many men were with you in the Hontvet cottage when you found that pencil, Emil?"

The boy hesitated. "Well, Sir, my father, and the sheriff, and the coroner's men."

"And, son, how many of them were writing down notes with red pencils?"

The boy turned crimson. "I can't say, Sir."

"Do you own a red pencil, Emil?"

"Yes, Sir."

"And do you occasionally chew on one end of it?"

Celia sighed. She had to concede that this time Tapley was right. She herself recently had used a red pencil to correct the galleys for her Shoals book. Karl had borrowed it, and he constantly gnawed on his pencils, though she told him not to. For one fleeting moment she was haunted by doubt, but, of course, Tapley was right. The red pencil could belong to anyone.

District Attorney Plaisted called Horace Chase, a Boston physician, as the final witness of the day.

"What is your occupation, Dr. Chase?"

"I specialize in the blood analysis of men and animals. The blood of humans has a peculiar corpuscle resembling a small India rubber ball that has been impressed by the finger and thumb, leaving a rounded edge and concave center. The animal corpuscle doesn't have this roundness. There are exceptions, of course."

"And could you please tell us what they are?"

"The camel, dromedary, and llama."

"Continue."

"If you take a thousand parts of blood, 903 are water, 80 albumen, 2 to 3 are fat, and 2 to 3 are organic substances not yet fully understood. The rest are mineral in nature."

"And how would you go about determining a blood sample?"

"If the blood were dry, it would be necessary to transform it to a fluid state. After that, the sample is examined under a microscope to see if the corpuscles I mentioned are present. If so, then mammalian or human blood also would be present."

"What other tools do you use for this examination?"

"A micrometer to count the corpuscles to the square inch. In man there are about 3,200. In a horse, 4,600, and so on. Even without this measurement you could tell the difference between, say, the blood of a fish and that of a human, because their forms are so different. For instance, fish corpuscles are egg-shaped.."

"Thank you, Dr. Chase. I think that gives us enough background. Now, did you examine the stains on the shirt on the exhibit table?"

"I did. As a matter of fact, I examined them ten times and the results were always the same. The blood on the shirt is human blood."

"Thank you, Dr. Chase. I defer to the defense for cross-examination."

Tapley crossed his arms and swaggered toward the man. "But, Mr. Chase, you say chemical testing in itself isn't reliable?"

"I do not. What I said is that if you find corpuscles with the micrometer, then you must make a chemical test to produce the coloring matter and —."

"And are you aware that authorities say it's impossible to distinguish between the blood of a horse and that of a man?"

"An experienced physician easily could make the distinction."

"Have I not heard that once the specimens are in a solution, the corpuscles enlarge? Forgive my ignorance, Mr. Chase, but I admit that I wouldn't know a human corpuscle if I met one on the street."

A few people laughed, but for the most part they were too engrossed in the testimony.

"Corpuscles can enlarge from day to day."

"If human blood can be enlarged, doesn't it follow that the blood of other animals also could enlarge?"

"Yes, but—."

"How many blood analyses have you made in criminal cases such as this, Mr. Chase?"

"Two or three."

"Two or three, Mr. Chase? That's not very many, is it?"

"No, but I've done hundreds of —."

Tapley turned away from the stammering man and faced the jury with an air of satisfaction. "You may step down, Mr. Chase."

19

The Alfred Hotel clerk peered at her signature. "Say, you aren't the woman who wrote those stories about the Isles of Shoals in *The Atlantic Monthly* awhile back, are you?"

She nodded.

"Nothing much ever happens in Alfred and now we got famous authors droppin' by. Just wait until I show the Mrs."

"Thank you," Celia demurred, not sure if he were complimenting her or about to ask to use her name for an advertisement.

He rang the desk bell and a matronly woman, her face flushed and a lock of hair dangling in her eyes, appeared wearing a house dress.

"Elsie, you'll never guess who this is."

Elsie looked Celia up and down and then craned over her husband's shoulder to gape at his pointing finger on the register. "Celia Thaxter!" she exclaimed. "Lord a mercy! I read every one of those Isles of Shoals stories. I couldn't put that magazine down."

Hotel guests seated in the front room turned to see what all the commotion was about.

"Mrs. Thaxter, what do you think? Did Louis Wagner do it?" she asked in a megaphone voice.

Celia wondered how she could possibly keep a low profile with this woman shouting her name to kingdom come. "I don't think we should discuss the trial, Mrs.—."

"Lovett. Elsie Lovett." The woman shook Celia's hand and leaned on the counter toward her. "Just between us women, I think Wagner's gentle as a lamb. And I'm an awfully good judge of character. You must have some opinion, Mrs. Thaxter."

"It's not opinion that sends a murderer to the gallows, Mrs. Lovett," Celia told her, thinking of how James Fields had asked her to write up the Shoals murders for the magazine. She'd agreed on one condition, that Louis Wagner be given a fair trail before one word of her story was published. There had been far too much speculation in the newspapers already, and she didn't want to jeopardize the man's chances.

The following morning the courtroom was packed again, though the crowd outside had diminished. Louis Wagner seemed calm and morose as he took the stand and placed his hand on the Bible. His black hair was slicked back with Brilliantine, leaving a wide expansive forehead above his penetrating eyes. He was neatly dressed in a jacket and bow tie, his beard trim, his moustache but a whisper outlining full sensuous lips.

If appearance were all, Celia could not imagine him as a murderer. But appearance wasn't all, and she, as much as anyone, realized that. When seated in a chair with a book, Karl appeared a scholar and gentleman. Yet, in fact, Karl was a vexing child who could make a nightmare of his and others' lives. So here was Wagner, seemingly abashed, meek and polite. He appeared innocent.

Defense lawyer Tapley began the questioning. "Mr. Wagner, tell the jury exactly where you were on the evening before your arrest in Boston."

In a well-modulated voice Wagner gave his testimony. "I am in Portsmouth at Johnson's boarding house. I go to the wharf at four o'clock and I see John Hontvet. He asks me to bait trawls when the bait comes on the train. I tell him if I'm around. I ask him how the fishing's going. He says all right. I ask if he's planning to buy a larger boat. He says, yes. But he's got a house of women and as fast as he make money they spend it."

Wagner paused like a vaudeville comedian waiting for laughter from the mostly male audience—and he got it.

"I eat at Mrs. Johnson's," he continued, "and at half past six I go to Caswell and Randall's fish store. A man comes and asks if I help load fish. I do and I blister my knuckles."

"A likely story," someone shouted.

Down went the gavel. "The next person in this courtroom speaking off the stand will be fined," Judge Barrows said. "Proceed, Mr. Wagner."

"I walk up Congress Street for a glass of ale. About eight I meet a man on the wharf who asks me to bait trawls. I bait about nine hundred hooks. Afterward, I have two more schooners of ale. On the corner of Court Street I get sick and heave up. There's a pump on the sidewalk and it's slippery. I fall and hurt my knee on the ice, but I manage to get back to Johnson's where I see John Hontvet baiting trawls."

"Did you speak to him?"

"No. I'm too tired and I fall asleep on the divan. Before daylight

I go down to the wharf again. It's low tide so I go back to Mrs. Johnson's and see her in the yard. She asks where I been. I tell her I'm there most of the night. At breakfast I see Mr. Kenniston and Mr. Moore. Then I go into the barroom to look at clock."

"And what time was it?"

"It's twelve minutes past seven."

Celia wished she were the lawyer; she had some questions of her own. If the Hontvets had to wait until midnight for bait from Boston, wouldn't the Portsmouth fishermen have to wait too? How could Wagner bait nine hundred hooks when the bait hadn't arrived until later that night? Also, why had Wagner said twelve minutes past, and not seven or seven-fifteen. Nobody looked at the clock that carefully.

And if he were feeling so badly, why hadn't he stayed home and gone to bed? The strongest fisherman on the Shoals stayed home when he felt poorly, knowing that he'd be useless in a boat or on the wharf. Then there was the point about his knuckles. Had he blistered and scraped them unloading the fish or baiting the hooks? There were altogether too many red herrings in his testimony.

"After breakfast I walk to Liberty Bridge and talk to the steamboat captain," Wagner continued. "Then I go back to Johnson's and find Mary in the kitchen."

"Mrs. Johnson's daughter?"

"Yes, Mary. I take her hand."

"You held her hand?"

"Yes, I like to hold ladies' hands." He smiled and again waited for laughter. But his lawyer flashed him a look of warning. "I tell her I feel badly and she says I'm drunk. I tell her I'm not. She tell me to turn in and I say I feel like walking it off."

"And you were talking with?"

"Mary Johnson. Then I take her other hand and she kiss me. I see Olava Johnson at the breakfast table and I kiss her too. I done it every morning. Anytime of day I receive it when I want it."

Hoots and whistles resounded through the courtroom, and while order was being restored Celia thought about Karen Christensen. Louis often had been with her. Is that why she'd wanted to go to Boston to live?

"I went to bakery, have a piece of pie," Wagner went on. "Then to the depot. I make up my mind to get on nine o'clock train for Boston. In Boston I walk down Hanover Street and go to Dutchman's store for a hat. I pay one dollar. I see a coat, pants, vest. He ask ten-fifty. But I give him ten.

"And then?"

"Then I go to Fleet Street and a shoemaker I know. I tell him I'm not fishing anymore because of rheumatism. I tell him I'm looking for work. The shoemaker's wife gives me a glass of kimmel. She wants that I buy boots with my silver piece but I tell her I have it a long time. I go to Mrs. Brown's and two ladies is there. I know one, but she says she don't know me. I jolt her memory by reminding her I am sleeping there last time and after I turn in she comes to my bed in her night shift. Then she remembers, and sits on my knee and asks if I'll stand her a treat. But I tell her I have no money. It's coming on next train. She ask me to stay and —."

Prosecutor Plaisted stood before the judge. "I object, Your Honor. This testimony isn't pertinent to the case, and there are women present."

The judge nodded. "Objection sustained. I suggest that the defense counsel alter his line of questioning."

"Yes, Your Honor." Tapley looked at his notes on the table, then faced Wagner. "What was this girl's name?"

"Emma. I don't know her other name."

"And have you seen her since?"

"Yes, Sir. In this courtroom."

People turned in their seats, trying to catch a glimpse of the notorious Emma Brown who had testified the day before. She was easily spotted in a lavender silk frock and pink frilly bonnet.

"And did you hear her testify?"

"Yes. But she's wrong. I ask her if she knows me and she says I'm Louis Ludwick. I tell her I have been with a sailor who's called that and he fell overboard. She must mistake him for me."

Tapley nodded his head in agreement. "Do go on."

"I go back to Brown's after supper and a policeman is waiting for me. He drags me to another room and ask how long I'm in Boston. I say five days, but I am confused and I mean five years off and on. They ask if I read the newspapers and I say no. They ask if I've killed women on Isles of Shoals and I tell them I like ladies and why would I do such a thing?"

"And when you were apprehended did you have a beard?"

"I tell you. I cut my whiskers because Boston is proper like, and my face she looks neater."

Tapley looked toward the jury for their reaction. "Please continue."

"Next morning the officers drag me along the street."

"What do you mean by dragged. Did they literally drag you?"

"Yes, Mr. Tapley, Sir. They drag me by the arms to some kind of house where they take my picture. John Hontvet come to the station and say, 'Damn you, Louis. You kill Anethe and Karen. Hanging's too good for you!'"

"So what came next?" Tapley prompted.

Wagner surveyed the spectators as if looking for a friend among them. "Marshall Johnson and Officer Entwistle take me to office in station and say to me they do everything to help me."

Judge Barrows interrupted. "Do you consider this relevant to the case, Mr. Tapley?"

"Yes, Your Honor. I wish to show the manner of dealing with the defendant."

"You may proceed."

"And what did Marshall Johnson propose?"

"He tell me that if I confess and say I'm drunk and not know what I'm doing, I will only get six to eight years."

A hubbub arose and the jurors looked startled. Celia struggled to disbelieve what she had heard. If plea bargaining actually had taken place, the State didn't have a chance of convicting Wagner.

Louis' voice trembled. "I tell Marshall Johnson I suffer the consequence because God's looking over me. Twice he save me when I'm in trouble. Once at sea I fall overboard and am rescue and once I fall into ship's hold and am cripple all over. But God he watch after me." The tall, dark man's voice broke, and his shoulders shook.

He took out a handkerchief, blew his nose, and struck a pose of self-determination. "Mrs. Hontvet see me and say, 'You want to kill me, too, Louis?' Then she asks me where is my tall beaver hat. I tell her I don't own a tall hat."

"And what happened at the pre-trial in South Berwick, Maine, Mr. Wagner."

"There's a man—"

Attorney Plaisted interrupted. "Your Honor, I strongly object. We aren't gathered here to determine what took place at another trial."

"Exactly what is your intent, Mr. Tapley?" Judge Barrows asked the lawyer standing at Wagner's side.

"I propose to show that this man, a stranger without counsel or friends, was told by the officers that he need not testify and that if he did he would be cross-examined. And yet, Mr. Wagner took the stand of his own accord and submitted to cross-examination without aid or benefit of counsel."

"Objection overruled. You may proceed, Mr. Tapley."

Pleased by the judge's decision, Tapley smiled at his client. "Is there anything you forgot to tell the officers in South Berwick?"

"Just that I saw three men baiting trawls in Randall and Caswell's fish store and they can vouch for me."

"Anything else?"

"Only that I talk with John Hontvet last year and he say he'd like to hang some Americans on lantern posts and skin 'em alive."

Here, Tapley looked the defendant squarely in the eyes as if to say, You're overdoing it, Louis. "Had you ever had any difficulty with Karen or Anethe Christensen?"

"No, Sir."

"Any difficulty with the Hontvets?"

"No, Sir." Wagner adopted a hangdog expression and bowed his head. "They was my only friends. They was kind as my Mother."

"How long before March sixth did you bait trawls for David Burke?"

"Eight days, I guess. I blister my hands. I blister thumb, too, hauling nets."

"Exactly how do you do that?"

Wagner took out his large handkerchief and tied it around the rail of the witness stand, pretending he was hauling in fish. "Mr. Burke's son give me a sail needle and I run it through my skin. The blood she spurts on my shirt."

"And before yesterday had you seen the shirt taken from the Johnson's privy?"

"No, Sir."

"Are these your boots?"

"Yes, Sir."

"Did you see any other boots like these when you bought them?"

"The store has many."

"Yes, pencils and boots have a way of getting around, don't they?" Tapley said, smiling as he held up the boots for the jury.

"Your Honor, I object," Plaisted said in an irritated tone.

"Objection sustained." The judge leaned on his elbows and gazed down at the defense lawyer. "Mr. Tapley, please keep your personal observations for the final statement."

"Yes, Your Honor. Now, the day you left Johnson's did you or did you not put your shirt in the privy?"

"I did not. I had none to spare."

"When you were searched what did the officers take from you?"

"Four dollars paper and copper, half a silver dollar, five cents in silver, a gold ring, and my clothes."

"And where did you get your boots?"

"In Portsmouth."

"The size?"

"Eleven. They have couple hundred just alike."

"That is all, Mr. Wagner."

Louis Wagner mistakenly started to step down but was retained by the officer standing behind the witness box.

A man sitting next to Celia leaned over and whispered to her, "Poor devil, he don't realize he et his dessert first." But she felt little compassion for Wagner. His smiles, tears, and snide remarks did not sit right with her and from first to last his story had been full of inconsistencies.

The State Prosecutor Plaisted took over where Tapley left off.

"You say there were a few hundred size eleven boots in stock?"

"Yes, Sir."

"You don't mean a few hundred different sizes?"

"No, Sir. About a thousand shoes all together."

"What time of night did the man pay you for baiting those trawls?"

"I got no watch."

"Had you seen the man before?"

"No."

"Have you seen him since?"

"No, Sir."

"And he paid in advance."

"Yes, Sir."

"How long did you have the silver five cent piece in your pocket?"

"About fifteen months."

"And what about the white button found on the bureau in your room, Mr. Wagner?"

"I never see it before. I'm thinking maybe it is belonging to Mr. Moore or Mr. Kenniston."

"What was the first room you entered at the Johnson's on March sixth?"

"The kitchen."

"Why didn't you go upstairs to bed?"

"I feel badly, and I think I get sick. I stay downstairs so I can heave outside. Besides, it is warm downstairs."

"Why didn't you crawl into bed with a hot water bottle?"

Tapley struck a fist on the table. "Your Honor, I object."

"Objection sustained."

Plaisted continued. "What did you tell Emma Miller about money?"

"She says to me—"

"I didn't ask you what she said. I asked what you said."

"She want me to stand her a treat. I say my money comes on the next train."

"And was that true?"

"It's not true, but I say so."

"You lied to her?"

"Just for fun, because I don't feel like standing her a treat."

"And are you lying to the jury just for fun, too, Mr. Wagner?"

"Your Honor, I object." Tapley pushed himself up with both hands.

"Objection sustained. Mr. Plaisted, what I told Mr. Tapley applies to you as well," the judge remonstrated. "Please keep within the line of questioning."

"At Portsmouth did the officers do their best to protect you from the crowds?"

"Yes, Sir."

"And since you were brought here, has there been any violence against you?"

"What do you mean?"

"Has anyone struck or hit you?"

"No, Sir."

"Would you be able to describe any building in the vicinity of the pump in Portsmouth where you said you took sick?"

"No."

"Is the street lighted with gas?"

"I think one gas light."

"But you were seen by no one?"

"It was late."

"Just one more question and you may step down. Is it not true that fishermen usually wear knitted bands from old socks around their hands to protect them from blistering? Nippers, I believe they're called."

"Yes, Sir."

"Why weren't you wearing nippers when you baited the trawls for Mr. Burke?"

"I lost 'em."

After Wagner stepped down, a James F. Babcock was called to testify for the defense. He was a chemistry professor at the Massachusetts College of Pharmacy in Boston and had examined blood samples for several capital crimes. Tapley sidled up to the professor. "Can it be said with certainty whether fish or human blood is on a garment?"

The grey-haired bespectacled man spoke in a high nasal twang. "Quite impossible, especially after the blood has dried a few days. The corpuscles of fish blood are oval. When they dry they shrink. When soaked again, they assume a shape that could be mistaken for human blood. I know of no discovery since 1861 that would authorize anyone to say for certain whether blood was human or from some other creature."

The last witness before the jury adjourned for deliberation was the coroner who was asked to describe what he found March sixth on Smutty-Nose. Details of the gruesome scene were repeated. Anethe on the floor with her face cut beyond recognition and blood all over her nightdress. Karen's body face down, her forehead split and her hair caked with blood. Blood on the door. Blood on the bed sheets. Celia put her hands to her face.

The jury listened intently as each lawyer read a closing statement. The prosecution focused primarily on Maren's testimony. She had been there. If her word was not enough to convince the jury, they had only to think of the silver piece once owned by Karen Christensen and later found in Louis Wagner's waistcoat, of the bloody shirt in Mrs. Johnson's privy identified by her daughter as belonging to Wagner, of the button given by Maren to Karen and later found in Wagner's pocket.

The defense urged the jury to consider that because the murders were heinous and unforgettable, Officer Entwistle and Marshall Johnson were under pressure to deliver a suspect whether he was the murderer or not. The jury also must remember that a tall beaver hat, which the murderer was to have worn, had not been found. And any number of people carried buttons and silver pieces in their pockets.

The jury recessed for several hours, reconvening in the late afternoon.

The judge struck his gavel and the courtroom hushed to a strange, tense silence. The court clerk addressed the jury: "Who shall be your spokesman?"

A distinguished gentleman in a tailored summer suit stood in the jury box and faced the judge.

"The prisoner will please rise," the clerk ordered.

Wagner stood with his back to them.

"Prisoner, look upon the jury. Gentlemen of the jury, look upon the prisoner. Is the prisoner guilty or not guilty?"

The spokesman glanced quickly at Wagner, then looked away. "Guilty."

"In what degree?"

"The first degree."

20

From early childhood on White Island, Celia had thought of the sea as a huge moat guarding their peaceful kingdom from mainland forces of danger. Her newest protégé, Childe Hassam, whom she felt certain was destined for glory, painted idyllic watercolor sketches of Appledore. His impressions of her sunny garden, the pastel sky and calm summer sea, revealed not a trace of the anxiety that led her to lock her door at night. But the fear was there, and most natives felt it.

Now in the midst of memories that seemed like yesterday, Celia struggled against an invisible bond. Where was she? In bed. But how had she gotten there? A chair creaked, and she saw Karl by the window, tossing and turning in his sleep.

With concerted effort she struggled to free her legs from the covers and swing them over the edge of the bed, but she sank back, abandoning herself to sudden vertigo. After a few seconds she swung onto her feet and leaned toward the bedstead. Groping for support, she lurched forward to the chair at her desk and waited for her head to clear.

She turned a small key in the center desk compartment and removed a packet of documents and letters. Avoiding the temptation to rest, once more she lunged for the bedstead, making her way to the side and propping herself on her hands until she could get back under the covers.

Strength regained, she drank some water and lighted a gas lamp beside her bed. One by one she looked through the assorted letters, hoping they would jolt her memory. Yes, now she remembered. She'd been worried about Karl. Levi had left their other sons a small inheritance but nothing for Karl, and she wanted to check her will to see if she had provided for him. It wasn't difficult to locate, being larger and more official looking than the rest. She glanced quickly through the formal legal transcription. Yes, she'd appointed Roland as executor of Karl's share to be held in trust until he needed it.

In her heart she knew she'd wronged Karl. Ever since Wagner was found guilty some twenty years ago, she'd blamed herself for letting that one instant of doubt cross her mind. But hadn't she also wondered where her brothers had been, and what they'd been doing the night of the murders?

Now she realized it wasn't a question of Karl's guilt but of hers. No matter how hard she tried, she never felt she'd done enough for him, and she desperately wanted to be forgiven for having brought such a helpless and troubled being into the world. She craved a sign that she was part of a plan, unfathomable, yet perfect in its illimitable knowledge of love and fulfillment. Levi would have called her a fool.

She shuffled randomly through the packet and came across a letter that looked vaguely familiar. Holding the dog-eared piece of folded paper to the light, she strained to decipher the feel of its history. A surge of silent joy came over her. Yes, now she remembered. John had given it to her in Amesbury. That sweet day.

During the past year, he'd written to ask that she destroy his letters, promising he would do the same. With sadness, she burnt them. How pleased she was that this one survived — she hadn't even read it!

Celia loved John. At first, she'd thought she was infatuated by his handsome dignity and personal charm, and had been extremely flattered by the famous poet's attentions. After awhile, she reasoned that their attraction must hinge on a shared interest in poetry, which was partially true, because his encouragement of her writing brought them closer together. But later, when she became a poet in her own right, and they still were seeing each other, she ran out of excuses.

As she looked at the letter, she remembered that he'd asked her to read it when she was troubled and in need of a friend. Under those conditions, she could have read it a hundred times over, and yet, here it was, tucked away and waiting as though for this moment.

Delicately, she opened the sheet of paper. It wasn't a letter at all. John's familiar handwriting awakened loving memories. She read his poem, and wept softly as she read it again.

Under the shadow of a cloud, the light
Died out upon the waters, like a smile
Chased from a face of grief. Following the flight
Of a lone bird, that scudding with the breeze,
Dipped its crank wing in leaden-colored seas,
It saw in sunshine lifted, clear and bright
On the horizon's rim the Fortunate Isle
That claim thee as its fair inhabitant,

And glad of heart, I whispered, "Be to her,
Bird of the summer sea, my messenger;
Tell her, if heaven a fervent prayer will grant,
This light that falls her island home above
Making its slopes of rock and greenness gay,
A partial glory midst surrounding gray,
Shall prove an earnest of our Father's love,
More and more shining to the perfect day.